MARVEL

THE AVENGERS™

MARVEL
AVENGERS™

THE AVENGERS
ASSEMBLE

ADAPTED BY Thomas Macri

Based on the Motion Pictures

Iron Man, Screenplay by
Mark Fergus & Hawk Ostby and Art Marcum & Matt Holloway

Iron Man 2, Screenplay by Justin Theroux

The Incredible Hulk, Screen Story and Screenplay by Zak Penn

Thor, Story by J. Michael Straczynski and Mark Protosevich,
Screenplay by Ashley Edward Miller & Zack Stentz and Don Payne

Captain America: The First Avenger,
Screenplay by Christopher Markus & Stephen McFeely

Marvel's The Avengers, Written by Joss Whedon

MARVEL
NEW YORK

MARVEL

www.marvel.com

™ & © 2012 Marvel & Subs.

All Rights Reserved. Published by Marvel Press, an imprint of Disney Book Group.
No part of this book may be reproduced or transmitted in any form or by any means,
electronic or mechanical, including photocopying, recording, or by any information
storage and retrieval system, without written permission from the publisher. For
information address Marvel Press, 114 5th Avenue, New York, New York 10011-5690.

Printed in the United States of America

First Edition

1 3 5 7 9 10 8 6 4 2

V 475-2873-0-12032

ISBN 978-1-4231-5397-9

THE FIRST AVENGER

STEVE ROGERS came of age in a time unlike any we had seen before and, hopefully, will see again. The entire world was at war. Worse, this was the second war of its kind in less than a quarter century. Steve's parents had served in that last war—the Great War, as it was called in Steve's day—and through them, he learned valuable lessons about what it meant to be a good soldier and, moreover, a good man.

By the time Steve was a teenager, the Second World War had been raging in Europe for years. And in 1941, just before Steve turned twenty-three, America joined in the worldwide fight. Steve had grown up watching the boys in his Brooklyn neighborhood line up at recruiting centers, suit up in uniform, pack their bags, and leave for deployment, many—*most* it sometimes seemed—never to return home. Every day, the streets outside his cramped four-story walk-up sounded less and less like games of stickball, skelly, and kick-the-can and more like the quiet of a church on a weekday afternoon. The gruff male voices that had filled the air gave way—slowly at first, then more rapidly—to the chatter of women on the home front: *Did you hear what happened to Tony McGrath? My Johnny hasn't written in weeks; he makes me so nervous, that boy. I just want James to come home, Jimmy, Jr., needs to meet his father.* . . .

Occasionally, a wail would pierce a quiet evening. Steve always knew what it meant—another Brooklyn boy gone forever. Did he know this one? He'd already stopped counting the friends he'd lost months ago. Nothing seemed to make sense anymore. The streets outside his window had changed. The nation and the world had changed. Nothing was certain except one very important thing: Steve had an irrepressible desire to fight—to help end this war so that throughout Brooklyn, America, and the entire world the sounds of laughter and games would replace the sobbing of those waiting for their loved ones to return home. He was going to fight to liberate the people who had been held prisoner by this war. He was going to fight to overthrow the madmen waging it. And he was going to fight to win the war so that after it was over not another drop of blood would be spilled.

So as soon as he was of age, Steve and a few other neighborhood boys, including his best friend, James "Bucky" Barnes, lined up at the local recruitment center to join the fight. Steve always felt small around the other boys, mainly because, physically, he *was*. Steve was much shorter than average, with a slight frame, and he weighed in at just under a hundred pounds. He had difficulty breathing the polluted New York City air and was easily winded. His cheeks looked hollow, and he was so thin that his eyes nearly bulged from his skull. But those same eyes revealed another side of Steve. He was filled with kindness, compassion, and a need to defend what was right and just.

If Steve had any power at all, it was not in his body, but in his soul.

The army, however, was not interested in what Steve believed in, so much as what he could *do*. And after a brief physical exam, they determined he couldn't do much. He'd be more of a liability on the battlefield than an asset. For Steve's own good, and the good of the other soldiers, the army refused to allow him to enlist.

"Don't worry, Steve," Bucky said. "You'll be safe here, and you'll be here to look after the old neighborhood while we're away."

Steve wasn't ready to give up. "I'm coming with you," he told Bucky.

Bucky laughed it off. "I know you want to do this, but . . ."

"But *nothing*, Bucky. This guy here didn't take me, I'll try somewhere else. Everyone's doing their part; I want to do mine."

The next week—and the week after that, and the next two weeks following—Steve tried his luck again, each time at a different recruitment center. But each time, he failed his physical. And though it seemed as if his luck would never change, Steve refused to give up hope.

The night before Bucky was set to leave for the army, he and Steve went out on a double date to the World Exhibition of Tomorrow—a World's Fair that was part science show and part amusement park. Bucky and the girls he'd brought along wanted to see the Stark

Industries exhibition. The world-renowned inventor Howard Stark was going to personally present some of his latest creations, including a car that could hover aboveground and ride the wind instead of the road. But despite the amazing display of futuristic technologies, Steve was focused on plans for his *own* future. He wandered away from the others and approached the exhibition's army-recruiting center.

Bucky stepped away from the girls and jogged over to Steve.

"You're really going to do this *now*?" Bucky asked.

"It's a fair. Figured I'd try my luck," Steve joked.

"As *who* this time?" Bucky asked. "Steve from Ohio? It's illegal to lie on your forms, Steve. They'll catch you. Or worse, they'll *take* you! This isn't some back-alley scrap. It's a *war*."

"It's *the* war," Steve said. "It's the war we can't lose. This is the one that counts, and I mean to be counted."

Bucky asked Steve to forget about enlisting—at least for now. It was Bucky's last night before shipping out. There were two pretty girls who wanted to go dancing waiting for them. Steve just smiled and shook his head. Bucky sighed, seeming to know that nothing would change his friend's mind. The two hugged, not sure if they'd ever see each other again, and each began a new journey. Bucky was off to war, and Steve was walking into the sixth battle of his own personal war—a battle to be allowed to fight.

After filling out a form with a list of questions he'd memorized by now, Steve was brought to the exam room. It was a scene he'd played out what felt like a thousand times. There was the exam table where they'd ask him to lay down so they could check his vitals. There were the tools that the doctor would use to perform the exam. The wastebasket in the corner, the eye chart on the far end of the wall. . . . The sign above his head read IT IS ILLEGAL TO FALSIFY YOUR ENLISTMENT FORM. The moment Steve saw the notice, an MP walked in.

Steve might have been weak and frail, but until this moment, he had never been frightened. It looked like the government was finally fed up with what they clearly saw as his games. Trailing behind the MP was an older, bearded man in a lab coat and glasses. He thanked the MP and dismissed him.

"So, five exams in five tries, in five different cities. All failed. You are very tenacious, yes?" The man said in heavily accented English. Was it a *German* accent that Steve detected?

Steve stuttered and tried to explain, but the man held up his hand.

"So, you want to fight?" the man asked.

"I don't like bullies," Steve answered.

"I can offer you a chance," he said.

Steve's eyes widened.

"Only a *chance*," the man repeated. He introduced himself as Doctor Abraham Erskine of the Special Scientific Reserve unit of the US Army. Steve wasn't sure what that meant, and he didn't much care. If Dr. Erskine had a way to get Steve into the army, he would take it—no questions asked.

For weeks, Steve trained at a boot camp with a core group of other men—as usual all of them were taller, healthier, and fitter than he was. Steve scrambled to run through obstacle courses, which he routinely failed to complete. He struggled to keep up during training runs, barely crossing the finish while the rest of the pack jogged hundreds of yards ahead. But Dr. Erskine could see something in Steve that others didn't—a fire in his eyes and a desire to do the right thing.

On Steve's final day at training camp, a grenade was dropped in the middle of the trainees.

"Grenade!" cried Colonel Phillips, who was in charge of the camp.

The soldiers scattered, finding cover behind tanks, inside ditches, under any shelter they could find. Every soldier fled.

Except one.

Steve jumped on the grenade in the hopes that he would save his fellow soldiers. He balled himself up on top of it and waited for it to explode. But it never did. It had been a test—the last and most important in a long line of them. And Steve had passed. For all his physical shortcomings, he had exactly it would take to become the best man the army had—a Super-Soldier.

Steve had always been a Super Hero in spirit, but now he would be one in body as well. The chance that Dr. Erskine had offered Steve was to take part in a clandestine experiment called Project: Rebirth. For years, the government had been working on a project that would deliver them a soldier who was stronger, more agile, and more adept than even their best men. Steve, having proved he had the heart, would be awarded the body.

The very next day, Steve, Dr. Erskine, Colonel Phillips and British agent Peggy Carter arrived in a secret lab under an old antiques shop in Brooklyn. Steve was awed by the secret nature of the place and the unbelievable technology in use there. He was escorted by Agent Carter through doors into the main area of the lab, where a crowd of scientists and government officials looked on skeptically—this weak and skinny fellow was America's greatest hope?

Agent Carter held her head high, encouraging Steve to ignore the group.

Steve didn't have the time or, frankly, the head, to worry about them. Not only was he used to people's disapproval, he had also recently gone from being an ordinary kid from Brooklyn to being a soldier in the company of some of the most brilliant scientific minds on Earth.

First, he'd met Dr. Erskine, and now Howard Stark—the famous inventor whose presentation he'd skipped out on months before at the exhibition. That night Steve only had one thing on his mind—joining the army. But now he couldn't have been more interested in Mr. Stark's creations. The most intriguing was one that looked like a steel capsule in the center of the lab. Mr. Stark and Dr. Erskine explained that Steve would be dosed with the Super-Soldier Serum, which would enlarge his muscles, and then he would be enclosed in Mr. Stark's tank and bombarded with vita rays. These would control his muscle growth and prevent him from going into shock or, worse, being subjected to unchecked growth. Mr. Stark explained that the lab was in Brooklyn because they needed to draw on as much energy as possible and the New York City power grid offered just that—at least he hoped it did.

Without hesitation, Steve allowed himself to be strapped to a table within the chamber. Soon its doors sealed shut around him. Mr. Stark pulled a lever, and several doses of serum were administered by Mr. Stark's device. Steve's vitals all registered normally as the first stage in the process was completed. Then Mr. Stark pulled a lever and turned a dial to administer the vita rays. He slowly and carefully increased the dose, closely monitoring Steve, and watching Dr. Erskine, who stood beside the chamber. As the radiation increased, Steve's heart began to race. It was clear that the stress was weighing on him. An unearthly wail came from inside the chamber—and some in the group called out to stop the experiment. But Steve hollered from his confines, telling them not to stop.

"Keep going," he yelled. "I can do this!"

Howard Stark continued to increase the vita rays. When the machine neared 100-percent capacity, the lights began to flicker—some even burst. The technicians scurried as a gradually increasing hum filled the lab as the raw energy being fed to Steve mounted. Finally, the wave culminated in a spectacular pop. The technicians, doctors, special agents, and everyone else in the room ducked for cover. Then the doors of the airtight chamber opened with a low hiss, and Steve emerged from within.

But it was no longer the same Steve.

Dr. Erskine and Agent Carter helped Steve from the chamber. As he stood up, he attempted to adjust to his new perspective.

"How do you feel?" Agent Carter asked.

"Taller," Steve replied.

Steve, who had entered the lab a sick and weak kid

was now the fittest soldier in the US Army. A feeling of joyous success permeated the room. But before any celebrating could commence, an explosion rocked the lab's control booth. Then, one of the observers pulled a gun from his jacket and shot Dr. Erskine in the chest.

Steve rushed to the doctor's aid, while the man who had shot him grabbed the last vial of serum and fled the scene. Agent Carter ran after him, while Steve tended to the doctor. With what appeared to be the last bit of strength he had left inside of him, the doctor, who had always told Steve he had the guts to be the world's best soldier, pointed to Steve's heart. He tried to speak, but couldn't. There was no need. Steve knew what he was telling him. The doctor let out a long, slow breath and went limp in Steve's arms. Steve let the older man's body down gently. Then, with all the amazing power he had just acquired, he rushed off to avenge the only man who had ever believed in him.

Steve ran faster than any human being ever had. He spotted the man he was looking for jumping into a car. Steve ran through traffic, leaped over fences, and rode on the roofs of moving vehicles so he wouldn't lose his target. On the Brooklyn waterfront, he finally caught up with the man he was pursuing. The man jumped into what could only be—as improbable as it was—a submarine. The ship submerged and Steve jumped in after it. In his new body, Steve was a strong swimmer, and he was able to catch up to the ship and wrench its pilot from the cockpit.

When Steve got them both to the dock, the man warned Steve that he and his agency HYDRA could not be stopped. "Cut off one head and two more shall take its place," the man said. "Hail HYDRA!" Then he bit down on a poison capsule and choked, taking his own life before Steve could question him any further.

When Steve regrouped with Colonel Phillips and Agent Carter, Phillips decided that it was best to keep Steve's new abilities a secret. Despite seeing Steve in action, he did not have faith in the idea that one man could turn the tide of the war. He had wanted an army of Super-Soldiers. One was not enough.

Steve was offered a different kind of military job —performing shows around the country as a character called Captain America. As "the Captain," Steve wore a bright red, white, and blue costume with a star emblazoned on the chest. His cowl was marked with a bold white A, and his feet and hands were covered in swashbuckling boots and gloves, and the costume was made complete by a coat-of-arms-shaped shield adorned with stars and stripes.

No matter what Steve was tasked to do, he did his best, and his stint as Captain America would be no exception. His shows were a huge success. The character began to appear in movie shorts, comic books, and stage shows. And sales of war bonds skyrocketed in every city where Captain America performed. He was doing his part, but he still felt like he should be doing more—especially given his abilities. He finally did get to the European theater, but not the military theater he'd been hoping for.

At a USO performance in Europe, Steve discovered that his best friend, Bucky, was part of a battalion that appeared to have been lost in battle. Steve was not one to disobey orders, but he knew that if Bucky was still alive, Steve might be his only chance. With Agent Carter's and Howard Stark's help, Steve disobeyed orders, boarded one of Stark's jets, and headed for the coordinates where Bucky's division had last been seen.

As they neared enemy territory, blasts sounded around Stark's plane and the craft began to rock. Steve told Stark and Carter to fly to safety—he was going in. He opened the hatch and leaped from the plane, parachuting through enemy fire and finally arriving at a HYDRA munitions factory.

Steve sneaked into the HYDRA plant, winding his way through the labyrinth of tanks and tubes. He took out a HYDRA agent, then another and another, and continued to do so as he made his way through the complex, looking for the POWs from Bucky's division. When he finally found the prisoners, Steve used all his strength to set them free. When the prisoners asked him his name, he told them he was Captain America.

Together with the freed prisoners, Steve battled his way through the compound. But as he was escaping, large areas of the building began to explode, and it wasn't the doing of any one of Steve's allies. Whoever was in charge must have been causing the building to self-destruct.

Still, Steve was not leaving until he found Bucky. He'd go down with the building if he needed to, but he would not give up. Blasts rocked the complex all around him. Fire and debris rained down as he darted through the corridors. He was sure he wouldn't survive this and was becoming even more certain that he wouldn't locate Bucky. But he was not going to stop trying.

While vaulting over a collapsing beam, Steve saw something through the smoke. It looked like the figure of a man laid out on a stretcher. Steve rushed over. It *was* a man, and as he struggled to help him, he realized the man was Bucky.

Steve helped Bucky to his feet. Bucky was woozy and confused, but able to walk.

"I thought you were dead," Steve told his friend.

Bucky looked Steve up and down.

"I thought you were smaller," Bucky responded.

The two quickly raced to escape the building before it was fully destroyed. They sprinted across burning corridors, through smoldering passageways, and over collapsing catwalks. Just when they caught sight of an exit only a few hundred yards away, a tall, imposing man blocked their path. As Steve met his eyes, he recognized him as Johann Schmidt, HYDRA's chief officer.

Schmidt threw a powerful punch at Steve. He hit so

hard that his fist made an impression in Steve's shield. The two continued to battle, and when Steve landed a punch on Schmidt's face, the HYDRA officer's skin appeared to slide out of place. It was as though his top layer of skin was nothing more than a loose-fitting mask. Every time Steve landed a punch on Schmidt's face, the skin shifted more, and what looked like raw muscle became more and more visible from underneath his mask.

Schmidt finally tore the layer of false skin from his face and revealed himself as he truly was—a man with a gruesome red skull for a head. The Red Skull turned and walked calmly from the crumbling building. He had a plan for escape. But Bucky and Steve were trapped. A huge explosion separated the two men, but both refused to leave until they knew the other was safe. They managed to reach each other, then looked for others who might be trapped in the building. After a sweep where they managed to rescue all the soldiers who were being held at the compound, they made their way back to base.

When they arrived, Steve found himself in the unfamiliar position of being respected, trusted, and admired.

Even Colonel Phillips, who up till this time had been tempering Steve's passion, was willing to give him the benefit of the doubt. He allowed Steve to assemble a squad to accompany him and set a goal of identifying and destroying all of HYDRA's bases.

In the months that followed, Steve became the man he always knew he could be—leading a troupe of Howling Commandos from theater to theater—Europe to the Pacific, and anywhere the enemy was hiding out in between. One by one, Captain America and his commandos eradicated every HYDRA base on the map. The army outfitted Steve with a unique suit—red, white, and blue, with utility and cargo pockets—and Howard Stark bestowed upon him an unbreakable vibranium shield, painted to match his uniform.

Then one day, on a particularly dangerous mission aboard a train running through the Alps, Steve lost his best friend. Bucky, struggling to hang on to the side of the train as it traveled over a gorge, fell from the side and plummeted into the abyss before Steve's eyes.

"Bucky!" Steve cried. But it was over.

Bucky's death caused Steve to press on even further, taking out HYDRA agents left and right. Steve believed HYDRA's motto was wrong, that there was one HYDRA head that, if cut off, would prove to be the death of the entire organization. He would not relent until he had the opportunity to combat it—the Red Skull.

Steve soon got his chance, when he cornered the Red Skull aboard a hulking HYDRA aircraft. The two men battled bitterly, and then Steve did something that turned the tide of the fight. He tossed his shield, which crashed into a lighted power supply in the center of the ship. The supply crackled with energy. Something was obviously very wrong.

"No! What have you done?" the Red Skull shouted. He picked up something that had fallen from the vessel—it was unlike anything Steve had ever seen. It was a glowing blue cube, and the Red Skull told Steve it contained unimaginable power. Steve wondered if this could be true—and if it were, could this be how the Red Skull was able to be so successful? Was he somehow harnessing the power of this cube?

The Red Skull lifted the cube, and the ship, the cube, and Schmidt himself began to pulse with power—too much power. A beam of blue light shot down from the heavens and absorbed Schmidt. The Red Skull and everything around him was vaporized. Everything but the cube itself, which burned all the way through the aircraft's thick metal and plummeted to the Earth below.

Steve rushed to gain control of the listing aircraft. He noticed on a monitor that the ship was loaded with explosives and locked on a target—New York City. It would be impossible to land, and even more difficult to deactivate the ships' weaponry. There was only one way to handle the situation. Steve radioed Agent Carter at base.

"Steve!" she shouted.

"This thing is moving too fast, and it's heading to New York. I've got to put her in the water. Right now I'm in the middle of nowhere; if I wait any longer, a lot of people are going to die. This is my choice."

Captain America grabbed hold of the controls. He steeled himself for what he knew would be a rough, and final, landing. He braced himself, fired the thrusters on the Red Skull's aircraft, and plunged the ship—and himself with it—into the frozen recesses of the Arctic Circle.

Not long after Steve's final flight, victory was declared in Europe and shortly thereafter on the Pacific front. The battles were won, the war was over. And so was the age of the Super-Soldier, the age of the Super *Hero*.

Or so it seemed.

CHAPTER ONE

BRUCE BANNER was about to change the world. For years he'd been studying the effects of gamma radiation. Even in his undergraduate studies, he'd persisted with a clear focus, surpassing many of his professors in their understanding of how the rays might be manipulated.

In his studies, he'd become more and more sure that the radiation, which had always been viewed in terms of their potential for weaponry, could benefit human cell defenses and combat the effects of harmful radioactive waves. In other words, he could use it to make humans immune to many devastating diseases.

Bruce was so sure of his work that he decided to use himself as a test subject. He sat in a specially designed chair that would help his physical body remain stable and still as he received his dose of gamma radiation.

The room sat apart from the control area, which was set off by a radiation-resistant glass provided by Stark Industries.

Bruce braced himself in excitement. He smiled and nodded toward the control booth, where colleagues who had also become close friends, including Dr. Betty Ross, were stationed. Also stationed there was General Ross of the US military, who was funding a large portion of the project. Bruce smiled and nodded, indicating that they should begin.

A low hum filled the room, and a green target moved slowly from the far end, over to the chair, gliding over Bruce and finally landing on his forehead, which is where the radiation would first be administered.

A green ray of energy streamed out toward him, and immediately Bruce felt altered. He'd never felt so good, so energized. But this was just the beginning. The dose of radiation was slow and steady, so he had a considerable amount of time left before the process was complete.

As the experiment continued, Bruce's strength grew, but in a way he hadn't anticipated. He glanced over toward the monitor that was tracking his heart rate.

It was escalating. At the same time, the power welling up inside of him was reaching a fever pitch. Something was wrong.

Bruce panicked. He began to struggle to release himself from the bonds that tied him to the chair. As his panic increased, he felt power—and anxiety and struggles—well up inside him and then flow straight to his head. His eyes popped open and everything looked clearer than he'd ever seen it before. His anxiety had subsided, but he felt an anger—a *rage*—taking hold. Something else was in control now—and it was inside of him.

His hands and arms began to pulse grotesquely as bone and muscle bubbled and morphed into something purely inhuman. Green waves undulated over his skin, and as his muscles swelled. The hue deepened, leaving his flesh a bright green. His body expanded to a point where his limbs could not be contained and popped right out of the restraints that were binding him.

He leaped up, now fully transformed into a green goliath. He stood over eight feet tall, and the width of his frame had more than doubled. He breathed heavily, hunched over, staring at the scientists and military personnel before him, no longer recognizing them as friends, colleagues, and supporters.

They looked on, too, paralyzed in sheer terror as they gazed at what Bruce had become—an incredible Hulk.

"My word . . ." General Ross uttered.

At that moment, the Hulk leaped through Stark's shatterproof glass window and crashed right through it. The gathered committee tried to flee, but nothing or no one was as quick as the Hulk, who tossed aside huge machines, tore through steel walls, and effortlessly swatted people aside.

The Hulk balled his fists and roared. He braced himself and aimed his head straight for a wall. Then he sprung up, held his forearm over his face, and crashed through metal, brick, and mortar to the outside world, where he could be free from these people who he could only identify as his captors.

CHAPTER TWO

PEACETIME WAS NOT usually very profitable for Tony Stark. This wasn't something he stressed over. Truth be told, something he didn't even realize just how much of a dip shares of Stark Industries' stock took when things were going well in the world.

Tony's late father, Howard, had left him the multi-billion dollar corporation in very healthy shape, so even in the worst of times, when the nations of the world were playing nicely, the company still did just fine.

Of course, Tony was a brilliant businessman, but his real love—other than partying—was technology. At age four he built his first circuit board, at six his first engine, and at seventeen he graduated suma cum laude from MIT. At age twenty one—a few years after Howard's passing—Tony became the CEO of Stark Industries.

Fortunately for shareholders, these were not the

worst of times for Stark Industries. True, the global economy had been sputtering, but America was involved in multiple wars and other overseas military operations. These conflicts required armor, vehicles, and weaponry, and Stark Industries was the nation's top supplier of military equipment and technologies.

And that's exactly what brought Tony to Afghanistan's Kunar Province. He was scheduled to meet with military officials to present the Jericho—the crown jewel in Stark Industries line of missiles and the first to incorporate their proprietary repulsor technology. The repulsors would ensure accuracy and exponentially increase the weapons' power.

Tony looked out over the arid landscape, turned to the gathered crowds, and nodded. With the press of a button, the Jerichos launched and began arcing overhead. Upon impact, the missiles leveled a crest of uninhabited hills and literally blew off the hats of the officers observing the demonstration.

And that's all there was to it. Twenty four hours worth of travel from Malibu to Afghanistan for a demonstration that lasted less than five minutes. Now it was time for a cool drink, then back into the convoy for another quick stop before boarding a private jet and heading home.

Tony hopped into his unglamorous armored vehicle and sipped his drink, as the convoy rolled away. For almost ten years, the area had been a hotbed of military activity. But as the convoy drove on, kicking up storms of sandy dust, Tony had a difficult time imagining that this place was in any way war-torn. They'd traveled miles through the rocky barren desert and hadn't passed another vehicle. Out his dirty window he'd occasionally see a man or two traveling who-knows-where with a mule or a camel in tow. Other than that, there was nothing but scrubby bushes and dusty mountains extending in all directions. Even in Tony's military Hummer, it was a bumpy ride filled with potholes and stones. The army-green metal interior and purely functional doors and windows were nothing like what he was used to back in the States, where his ride was fully loaded.

Tony adjusted his cuff links and twirled the ice in his glass. He'd miraculously managed to keep his custom-tailored suit spotless in spite of the filth of this place. The three young, heavily-armed soldiers who were escorting him had not said a word since they hit this poor excuse for a road. The officer sitting next to him looked over at Tony and then looked quickly away. Tony, bored, hot, and nervous that his clean suit would not stay that way much longer, decided to have some fun.

"I feel like you're driving me to a court martial. This is crazy. What did I do? What? We're not allowed to talk?" Tony asked.

"We can talk, sir," The soldier said.

"Oh, so then it's personal?" Tony said sarcastically.

"No, you intimidate them," the driver responded.

Tony was taken aback by the driver's voice. "You're a woman! I honestly . . . I couldn't have called that. I mean, I'd apologize, but isn't that what we're going for here? I mean, I thought of you as a soldier first."

"I'm an airman," she responded.

"Well, you actually . . . You have excellent bone structure there. I'm kind of, I'm actually having a hard time *not* looking at you now," Tony flirted. "Is that weird?"

The officers, including the driver, giggled.

"Ah, come on, it's okay. Laugh!" Tony said, smiling. "Anything else?"

The quiet soldier shifted uncomfortably.

"Um, is it cool if I take a picture with you?" he asked.

"Yes," Tony replied. "It's very cool."

The soldier shyly pulled out his camera and handed it to the officer in the driver's seat. He smiled and leaned in toward Tony, who flashed his camera-ready smile. The officer in the front seat fumbled with the camera, trying to figure out which button to press. The quiet soldier responded, "Come on! Just snap it, don't change any of the settings . . ."

At that very moment, just as the soldier was clicking the snapshot, the truck at the head of the convoy—the truck directly in front of Tony's Hummer—exploded into a fiery ball of white-hot flame.

The soldiers started to shout, and Tony, clearly shaken, asked what was happening.

"Just stay down!" the soldier sitting next to him shouted. Then he, the driver, and the third escort jumped from the vehicle and opened fire to protect Tony.

Tony squatted down under the backseat of the vehicle. So much for the clean suit. Rapid gunfire sounded outside, and he could tell that his escorts were fighting a losing battle. Tony looked up just as a barrage of bullets riddled the armored doors with holes. Tony heard the windshield shatter and felt glass falling all around him. He looked up and saw soldiers falling in front and behind his vehicle. He knew he wouldn't make it out alive if he stayed in the truck, so he threw open the door and jumped out.

Bullets, shrapnel, and fire rained down around him, and he lunged into the air dodging them, taking shelter behind a large rock. Sounds of warfare popped and echoed all around him as he grabbed for his cell phone. He frantically started to key in a phone number, trying to call someone, anyone—but before he could finish dialing a wailing rocket soared overhead, and landed just a few feet away from Tony. His eyes widened as he noticed the stenciling on the side of the beeping time bomb, which read: STARK INDUSTRIES.

A fraction of a second later, Tony was enveloped in white flame, blown off the ground, and thrown harder than he thought possible a hundred meters from the blast site. Tony was barely conscious. He struggled to tear open his shirt, and realized that his Stark Industries Kevlar vest had been compromised. He was losing blood quickly and finding it impossible to keep consciousness. Finally, his head hit the ground and then everything faded to white.

CHAPTER THREE

TONY WOKE SLOWLY in a dark room, his head throbbing, his vision blurred. He couldn't see past whatever it was that covered his eyes. A bandage? No, it was too rough. As the ringing in his ears began to abate, he heard voices speaking a language he didn't recognize. The wrappings over his eyes seemed to cover his entire head. It was rough, like burlap. Come to think of it, it *was* burlap. His hands were burning. No, not burning— numb. He couldn't feel anything but a tingling in them. He couldn't move them. Or his feet. He was tied.

With a quick whip, the burlap hood was pulled from his head, and the little bit of light in the room stung his eyes. As he adjusted to the dimly lit room, he could make out what felt like sticks prodding him. But as things came into clearer view he realized they weren't sticks, but guns—rifles, machine guns.

The men surrounding him were hooded, threatening, menacing. And it was clear they had Tony's life in their hands. He looked down and noticed that his chest was bandaged with gauze. The room was still blurry, and he was having trouble focusing. He lost consciousness over and over again and had no idea each time how long he had been out. But during this time, he experienced nightmarish flashes of crude operations being performed on him. He felt sharp stabs of pain, and felt like he was being torn apart and stitched back together over and over.

Then he enjoyed a long period of rest, without these visions, and finally awoke in a cool, dark room. A hose had been placed up his nose while he was unconscious—to help him breathe or to drain blood, he figured. So whoever it was that did this to him clearly wanted him alive. He slowly pulled the hose from his nostril and attempted to sit up on his makeshift cot.

As he shifted, mechanisms rattled, and he realized he was connected to something. He turned and saw—a car battery, with wires running toward his chest? Tony tore the gauze off his chest and discovered what looked like a very simple transistor affixed there.

At the far end of the room, an old bespectacled man stood stirring a pot of something over a fire.

"What did you do to me?" Tony rasped.

"What I did is to save your life," the man replied with a pleasant smile. "I removed all the shrapnel I could, but there's a lot left near in your atria's septum. I've seen a lot of wounds like that in my village. We call them the walking dead, because it takes about a week for the scraps to reach their vital organs."

"What is this?" Tony asked pointing to the apparatus on his chest.

"That is an electromagnet, hooked up to a car battery. And it's keeping the shrapnel from entering your heart."

Tony shrugged uncomfortably and zipped up the sweater he found himself clothed in.

The steel door on the far side of the room rattled, and the man looked up, nervous. Then he snapped at Tony with a quick urgency.

"Stand up!" he told Tony. "And do as I do!"

The door opened and a dozen or so armed enemy soldiers entered. One walked in front of the others. He was large and carried papers in his hands. Tony figured he was the guy in charge here. He spoke in a foreign tongue to the man who had been helping Tony. The man translated that the enemy soldier wanted Tony to build him one of the Jericho missiles he'd demonstrated upon his arrival in Afghanistan. The enemy army had a stockpile of Stark Industries weapons. Tony could use those for parts and then supply a list of anything else he would need to build the missile. And when the missile was completed, the man would set Tony free.

"No, he won't," Tony mumbled under his breath, at the same time tentatively shaking the enemy's hand.

"No, he won't," Tony's companion agreed.

The two men were returned to the cave and were set to work.

"I'll be dead in a week," Tony said.

"Then this is a very important week for you," his companion replied.

Tony got to work immediately. He barked orders for everything he'd need for the project. And light—he needed more light to be able to work effectively. Men rushed in and out of the cell with munitions, wiring, batteries—all supplied somehow or other by Stark Industries.

Tony and his partner, whose name he learned was Yinsen, worked tirelessly, welding, soldering, melting metals in ingots and pouring it into molds. They rarely rested. But when one of them *was* resting, the other was always working. They established a twenty-four-hour operation, all while they were under the trained eye of their captors, who observed them through webcams strategically placed throughout the cell.

Their captors knew all about war, but nothing about science. So when Tony completed his first project, they had no way of knowing that the result was a palladium-fueled Arc Reactor. He would use it in place of the unreliable battery-powered magnet that was keeping him alive. It could power his heart for fifty lifetimes. . . .

Or it could power something huge for fifteen minutes.

Tony had a plan.

He unrolled a series of blueprints. The paper was transparent enough to see through the overlapping sheets. Tony shifted them strategically, so that a portion of each blueprint overlapped another—like a complex jigsaw puzzle. Yinsen raised his eyebrows as he examined the prints. It was like nothing he'd ever seen before. And it certainly wasn't the Jericho missile that their captors were expecting.

CHAPTER FOUR

TONY AND YINSEN worked furiously to complete their project. Tony's blueprints showed a huge suit of armor, powered by his Arc Reactor. The armor was large and thick enough to keep whoever was inside it protected, and it was fitted with simple but effective weapons. The reactor should have been able to power it long enough for Tony and Yinsen to make a clean getaway.

But as the suit began to take shape—the chest plate intact, the legs operating—even the captors, who didn't know much about science, began to suspect something was up. The materials that the duo were developing looked nothing like the Jericho blueprints. The captors stormed into Tony and Yinsen's cell and demanded an explanation.

Tony and Yinsen explained that it was a very

complicated project. Building a missile was not easy. The enemy guard was not buying it.

"You have till tomorrow to assemble my missile," the leader of the enemy unit snarled. Then he stormed from the cell and locked the two engineers inside once again.

Tony and Yinsen worked more furiously than before, and in a matter of hours it was ready to use. Yinsen quickly helped Tony suit up in the clunky armor. It looked like a huge iron tank, with a medieval-style mask and makeshift munitions. As soon as Tony was suited up, he made sure to stay out of view from the surveillance cameras to avoid arousing suspicion. It worked, with the captors noticing that Tony was missing right away. They rushed down to the cell to investigate.

The guards called through the door to Yinsen, asking where Tony was. But they were speaking a language that Yinsen wasn't familiar with. Yinsen called out to them using the few words he knew in order to hold off the men, but they threw open the door to storm in.

A huge blast rocked the entrance to the cell the

moment the door clicked open. Yinsen and Tony had rigged it to buy themselves time in the event that they were interrupted while assembling the armor. The blast rocked the compound, and the remaining enemy troops stormed down to the cell. Tony and Yinsen could hear the approach of their stomping feet and rattling ammunition as the two men anxiously finished preparing the suit.

As the soldiers marched closer, Yinsen realized that he and Tony would not be able to power up the suit before the men arrived. "We need more time," he said. "I will buy you more time. . . ."

He grabbed a machine gun from one of the fallen guards and stormed out of the cell, hollering. The soldiers were taken aback and held off approaching the cell. But they soon located Yinsen and surrounded him. Every one of the soldiers' guns was pointed at him. A chorus of clicks sounded. Just before they were about to shoot, the lights in the compound cut out.

Tony's suit had powered up, and in doing so had drained all the electricity in the complex. The soldiers scouted the area, not sure how or if to proceed. They carefully made their way down the corridor, feeling their way as they went. Some eventually arrived at the cell. They entered apprehensively, unsure of what awaited them.

And that's when Iron Man attacked.

Tony stepped from the darkness into the few shafts of light that made their way into the cell. Glimpses of the suit were visible, but the soldiers couldn't make out exactly what they were up against. As Tony stepped from the room, that all changed.

Tony's armor was a monolithic suit of metal, fitted with special devices. The enemy soldiers fired relentlessly, but their bullets couldn't penetrate Tony's suit. They ricocheted off and boomeranged back toward his attackers. Tony walked, undeterred, toward the open air, and as he did more and more soldiers descended upon him. But no matter their number, they couldn't stop Iron Man from moving forward. The heavy suit caused Tony to walk in a lumbering way, but that didn't prevent him from getting where he needed to go.

When he was almost at the exit, he found Yinsen. But he was badly wounded and laying on the ground.

"Yinsen!" Tony called out. "Come on! We've got to go! We have a plan, we've got to stick to it."

When the safety of the world is threatened, Nick Fury must assemble Earth's Mightiest Heroes—the Avengers.

Billionaire inventor Tony Stark was the perfect candidate for Fury's Avengers Initiative.

Fury recruited Stark for his genius, his repulsor technology, and his Iron Man armor. But he would need others.

Next on Fury's list was the Asgardian warrior known as the Mighty Thor.

Thor carried his hammer, Mjolnir, and had the ability to control lightning.

Years ago, weak and small Steve Rogers became Super-Solider
Captain America!

Armed with his indestructible shield, Cap was ready to rejoin
the fight for justice.

Fury needed someone who specialized in gamma radiation, so he recruited Dr. Bruce Banner.

When angered, Banner transforms from a brilliant scientist into the green goliath known as the Hulk.

Fury also wanted S.H.I.E.L.D. agents on his team, including expert marksman Clint Barton, aka Hawkeye.

Fury called upon agent and superspy Natasha Romanoff, aka Black Widow.

Agent Phil Coulson, Fury's right-hand man—always the first one on the scene and the last one out—was also enlisted.

Last but not least was Agent Maria Hill, who kept Fury in check and the Helicarrier in the air.

The Avengers would be put to the test against the Asgardian
Trickster–Loki!

"This was always the plan, Stark," Yinsen said with the little bit of life he had left in him. "Don't waste . . . Don't waste your life, Stark. . . ." This plea was the last that Yinsen uttered.

Tony turned angrily toward the exit of the cave that housed the compound. He lumbered forward and stepped outside. As soon as he did, the enemy unleashed all their fire on him. He must have been hit with hundreds—or thousands—of rounds of ammunition, but nothing penetrated his armor. When the enemy paused their fire, Tony challenged, "*My* turn," and lifted his giant metal arms.

Streams of fire flowed from his suit, igniting the air around him and forcing back his opponents. Tony turned his streams of fire toward the Stark Industries stockpile that the enemy army had amassed outside the cave. The weapons began to burn, and Tony knew it wasn't long before they would detonate. He lifted a flap under the cuff of his armor and pressed a red button. The suit began to rattle, and then it shot like a rocket high into the air, arcing away from the site. Tony could hear the ammunition exploding below him. He was a few hundred feet in the air when he felt the suit begin to sputter. Tony flailed his arms and legs, struggling to find some way to stay aloft. Then the power cut out altogether and Tony plummeted down into the vacant expanse of the Afghan desert, far from where anyone might find him.

CHAPTER FIVE

TONY WANDERED the desert under the oppressive heat of the Afghan sun for weeks. Or was it hours? Perhaps it was days, or years . . . Minutes, seconds, hours—everything was running together. The desert wind whipped at his feet and blew him every which way, like sand in a jostled hourglass.

He needed water. He needed food. He needed rest. But if he closed his eyes for a second, he might never open them again.

Tony ambled about as he attempted to keep his footing. But it was becoming more difficult to control his muscles, and the dunes' uneven surfaces were complicating matters.

Tony began to lose his focus. In his disorientated state, the whole world seemed to be turning white. He couldn't tell where the sand ended and the sky began, or

if the shimmering he observed on the horizon was a for-
giving pool of water or a cruel mirage. Above him, sound
seemed to swirl like the amplified beating of vulture
wings, or the hungry moan of an angel of death. As
the sound grew louder, Tony could feel the wind pick
up. He looked up and was sure that he saw huge dark
figures soaring overhead.

Tony squinted, then he filled with hope. These were
no birds or supernatural beings, they were US military
choppers! Tony felt a burst of adrenaline. He began to
jump up and down, waving his arms furiously, acutely
aware that this could be his only chance to be rescued.

The whirlybirds banked and swooped back toward
Tony, who broke down in hysterical laughter, delirious
from the heat and fatigue. The copters landed and a
dozen soldiers rushed out. They held their weapons at
the ready, but they began to drop them as they drew
closer to Tony. He collapsed onto his knees at the sight
of his close friend James "Rhodey" Rhodes, who was
an officer with the US Air Force.

"Next time, you ride with me, okay?" Rhodey said.

Tony grinned, only half conscious, and Rhodey
pulled him close, happy to see his friend alive.

It was a long ride back. On the way, Rhodey helped Tony rehydrate and cleaned him up a bit. Once they arrived at base, Tony was fully examined and sutured up. Rhodey had known well enough to have one of Tony's tailored suits ready for him, and Tony shaved and made himself look as dapper as he could. Even beat up and bruised, Tony looked every bit the billionaire playboy he was. It was just his way.

Rhodey helped him to into a wheelchair and they boarded an Air Force jet for their long journey home. Tony mostly slept on the flight. After months in captivity and who-knows-how-long wandering the desert, the voyage didn't seem all that terrible. When the jet landed and the gangplank descended, Tony was even able to step up from his chair, supported by Rhodey. As the two men walked slowly down the gangway, a medic approached them with a stretcher.

"Are you kidding me with this? Get rid of it," Tony said dismissively.

Crowds of military personnel below were awaiting his arrival, but Tony locked eyes on the one person besides Rhodey that he had actually been concerned about never seeing again.

"Hm. Your eyes are red," he said as he approached the woman, who with her suit, pulled-back hair, and made-up face looked as out of place as Tony on the airfield. "A few tears for your long-lost boss?"

"Tears of joy," Pepper Potts joked. "I hate job-hunting."

"Yeah, vacation's over," Tony said.

The two of them entered a waiting car.

"Where to, sir?" The driver asked.

"Take us to the hospital please," Pepper responded to Tony's driver, "Happy" Hogan.

"No." Tony cut her off.

"No? You have to go to the hospital; you have to see a doctor; the doctor needs to look at you. . . ."

"'No' is a complete answer. I don't have to do any-thing. . . . I've been in captivity for three months, there are a few things I *want*. Two. One, I want an American cheeseburger, and the other is I want you to call for a press conference now."

"Call for a press conference? What on earth for?" Pepper asked, still arguing with her boss.

"Hogan, drive. Cheeseburger first," Tony demanded.

* * *

After a quick stop at a burger joint, Tony's car wheeled up to Stark Industries headquarters. The roar of applause from his staff was deafening as Tony stepped from his vehicle. And one man, Tony's second-in-command, Obadiah Stane, ran to Tony and embraced him.

"Hey, hey! Look who's here!" Obadiah said joyfully, hugging Tony tight. He ushered Tony past cheering crowds of Stark employees and hoards of media and press.

Pepper Potts looked on, relieved to have Tony back in mostly one piece. She smiled as camera bulbs flashed and members of the press swarmed around her boss.

Almost unseen, a suited man approached and stepped up beside her.

"Ms. Potts?"

"Yes," Pepper replied.

"Can I speak to you for a moment?"

"I'm not part of the press conference, but it's about to begin right now."

He handed her his credentials. "I'm not a reporter. I'm agent Phil Coulson with the Strategic Homeland

Intervention, Enforcement, and Logistics Division."

"That's quite a mouthful."

"I know, we're working on it. . . ."

"You know, we've been approached already by the DOD, the FBI, the CIA . . ."

"We're a separate division with a more specific focus. We need to debrief Mr. Stark about the circumstances of his escape."

"I'll put something on the books, shall I?"

"Thank you," Agent Coulson said, then he stepped away as Obadiah Stane took the podium.

Tony sat with his back against the front of the podium. He unwrapped his cheeseburger.

"Hey, would it be all right if everyone sat down?"

The gathered crowd looked around at the chairless room.

"Just sit down. That way, you can see me and I can . . . It's a little less formal. . . ."

Obadiah stepped out from behind the podium and sat down on the stage next to Tony.

"Good to see you," Tony said to Stane, who smiled back broadly.

"What's up with the love-in?" Rhodey whispered to Pepper.

"Don't ask me, I don't know what he's up to," Pepper responded.

Tony turned to the audience and began his press conference.

"I never got to say good-bye to my father. I never got to ask him about what this company did. If he was ever conflicted, if he ever had doubts. Or maybe he was every inch the man we all remember from the newsreels.

"I saw young Americans killed by the very weapons I created to defend them and protect them. And I saw that I had become part of a system that is comfortable with zero accountability."

Obadiah glared at Tony, and the audience, which Tony had clearly made uncomfortable with his frankness, began to cautiously ask questions.

"What happened over there?" a young reporter asked.

"I had my eyes opened. I came to realize that I have more to offer this world than just making things to blow up, and that is why, effective immediately, I am shutting down the weapons-manufacturing division of Stark Industries . . ."

The room exploded in an uproar of gasps and questions. Obadiah stepped up to the podium, smiling as broadly as he had since Tony arrived home. Pepper and Rhodey looked on slack-jawed as Tony, now standing as well, was swarmed by reporters.

Obadiah attempted to usher Tony off the stage, but Tony persisted. "Until such a time as I can decide what the future of this company should be, what direction it should take, one that I'm comfortable with and is consistent with the highest good for this country as well."

Tony stepped off the stage and out of the room, and Obadiah quickly grabbed the microphone, still wearing his broad smile but scrambling for a way to manage the situation.

"Okay!" Obadiah began. "What we should take from this is that Tony's back! And he's healthier than ever. We're going to have a little, um, internal discussion, and we'll get back to you with a follow-up."

CHAPTER SIX

OVER THE NEXT few weeks, things got very interesting for Tony. Obadiah Stane was not in the least happy with Tony's decision to close down Stark's weapons-manufacturing division. But Tony didn't care what Obadiah or anyone else thought about it. It was Tony's company, built by his father, and no one could tell him what to do with it.

Even after shares of Stark Industries' stock plummeted 57-percent, Tony refused to budge. He'd had a change of heart in Afghanistan, both figuratively and literally. Yinsen's struggle and sacrifice had opened Tony's eyes. He had talent and money and a fantastic scientific brain. Why, then, shouldn't he be helping the world as opposed to hurting it?

Tony spent most of his time rebuilding the suit he had developed in Afghanistan. Only this time it wouldn't be big and clunky, but as sleek and stylish as Tony himself. He was tireless in his efforts to get the jet propulsion just right so he could fly effectively. He strengthened the Arc Reactor that powered his heart and the suit. And he developed repulsor disks—much like the ones he'd used on the Jericho missiles—that would be affixed to his palms and could be used to fight off adversaries.

Ultimately, Tony had created the perfect tech suit. After a test flight, Tony's virtual butler, J.A.R.V.I.S.—who had the run of Tony's house and vied with Pepper for the most important position in Tony's life—suggested making the armor gold. Tony felt it was too flashy. He suggested adding splashes of red—and with that, Tony's suit's trademark red and gold colors were decided.

Now one of Tony's inventions wouldn't be used to hurt people, but to help them. Tony stepped into his newly refined suit and decided to take it for a ride. J.A.R.V.I.S. warned Tony that he might want to test the suit further before flying around the skies over California, but Tony was never one to shy away from adventure.

Tossing caution to the wind, he zoomed out of his house and into the night sky—shaky at first, but very quickly getting the hang of it. He swooped over the city, over the sea, and around office towers—it was the most amazing feeling Tony had ever experienced.

Once he became comfortable in his suit, he quickly put it to good use. His first mission would be the most obvious—he planned to return to Afghanistan, to the area where he'd been held captive, and help the people in Yinsen's village. Tony was successful on this first mission, but unfortunately he caught the eye of the US Air Force—and his friend Rhodey. The military wasn't happy about the idea of a maverick fighting unauthorized on war-torn foreign soil.

Worse, his actions caught the attention of Obadiah Stane, who was fed up with Tony and, it came to light, had been for some time now. Tony discovered that Obadiah was the person who had set up his kidnapping in Afghanistan. Obadiah wanted Tony out of the way so he could take control of Stark Industries. And he would stop at nothing to achieve that goal. Obadiah flew back to Afghanistan to retrieve Tony's original armor, improve on it, and create an armor bigger, more powerful, and fitted with an unimaginable array of weapons.

Obadiah soon had his suit. It was the very thing he needed to finish off Tony. It was three times as large as the Iron Man suit. Obadiah attacked Tony at Stark Industries. After a long battle, where Obadiah often had the upper hand, Tony, with the help of Pepper, overloaded the building's tremendous Arc Reactor and blasted Obadiah off the roof.

The power surge caused blackouts all over the city and sent a stream of light into the sky over LA so bright that it lit up the night like a noontime sun. This one was not going to go unnoticed.

Tony had won his battle, but he sure had some explaining to do.

CHAPTER SEVEN

TONY STEPPED UP to the podium. He had been briefed by Pepper, his PR team, Rhodey, and Agent Coulson of S.H.I.E.L.D. The story reported to the public was to be that there had been an electronic malfunction at Stark Labs the night before and a robotic prototype malfunctioned and caused damage to the Arc Reactor. With all of the fantastic innovations that Stark Industries had produced, the hope was that this story would fly.

S.H.I.E.L.D. had covered up Obadiah's demise, writing it off as a small-craft accident while Stane vacationed. With Rhodey setting the stage for Tony's press conference, Mr. Stark, as smooth as ever, was set to explain away the events of the previous night. The newspapers were calling the armored figure "Iron Man," and the name was taking hold. Tony liked it, and thought it was catchy—if a little inaccurate, since the suit was not iron, but a powerful alloy. Still, Tony was prepared to brush off "Iron Man" and preserve his secret identity.

"Uh, it's been a while since I've been in front of you; I figured I'll stick to the cards this time," Tony began.

The audience, many of them reporters who had attended Tony's previous press conference, rippled with laughter. Tony cleared his throat.

"There's been speculation that I was involved in the events that occurred on the freeway and the rooftop. . . ."

"I'm sorry, Mr. Stark," a female reporter cut him off, "but do you honestly expect us to believe that was a bodyguard in a suit that conveniently appeared *despite* that fact that you . . ."

"I know that it's confusing; it is one thing to question the official story and another thing entirely to make wild accusations or insinuate that I'm a Super Hero."

"I never said you're a Super Hero."

"You didn't?"

"Uh-uh."

"Well, good, because that would be outlandish and, uh, fantastic. I-I'm just not the hero type. Clearly. With this laundry list of character defects, all the mistakes I've made, largely, um, public."

Rhodey whispered to Tony to stick to the script and Tony nodded.

"The truth is," Tony continued, then paused, with his eyes locked on his cue cards for an eternal instant.

"I am Iron Man."

ASGARD

One could say that the Realm of Asgard is far from Earth, but that would not be entirely accurate. For the distance between Asgard and Earth is measured not in meters or miles. The journey from one point to the other cannot be traveled by placing one foot before the other, or by flying an aircraft. The two exist on opposite sides of the Bifrost wormhole.

It is much easier for Asgardians to travel to Midgard, which is what Earth is called on Asgard, then it is for Earthlings to travel to Asgard. Asgardians can travel relatively easily between Realms. And if Asgardians can do something, you can be certain they will. So, to put it plainly, the people of Asgard have, and still do, travel to Midgard. They do this by journeying over the Bifrost, the Rainbow Bridge that can transport them to any of the Nine Realms.

With the long history of intimate contact between Asgardians and humans came some misunderstandings.

Humans have called the beings of Asgard everything from demons and monsters to angels and gods for the abilities they possess. Asgard has found a place in human literature, history, culture, and lore. Thursday, to take one example, is named for Thor, son of Odin, Allfather of Asgard.

Like any father and son, Odin and Thor enjoyed a complex relationship. Odin loved his son and wanted what was best for him. But Thor was stubborn, proud, and arrogant. On the day that Odin was to bequeath the throne to Thor, a great banquet was held with all Asgardian royalty present—including Thor's mother, Frigga, and his younger brother, Loki. The kingdom was at peace with its neighbors, and all were set to celebrate with a great feast. Thor's closest companions were in attendance as well: Fandrall, Volstagg, and Hogun—together called the Warriors Three—and the Lady Sif, a proud and skilled warrior.

At the very moment that Odin was to bestow the crown unto Thor, a chill frosted the throne room's very air. The Asgardians looked about them. A chill like this—one that stabbed at your bones—was not common in Asgard, and it could only mean one thing. Frost Giants must be near. The icy blue inhabitants of Asgard's oldest enemy, the land of Jotunheim, must have somehow entered the Realm despite the truce between the kingdoms.

Odin, Thor, and Sif rushed from the throne room to the Vault, where all the greatest treasures of Asgard were kept. Sheets of ice covered the walls, and the Vault's sentries had fallen prey to an onslaught of ice. A giant suit of armor known as the Destroyer, powered by Odin's very life force, stood at the far end of the Vault. The Destroyer's only directive was to protect Asgard and its people. When a threat was posed, the Odinforce within the Destroyer would burn bright and lay waste to the threat. It had done that now—and recovered what the Frost Giants had intended to take: the Casket of Ancient Winters. Laufey, king of Jotunheim, once tried to use the casket to cover all Nine Realms with ice, so that he might rule over them. Odin and the Asgardian armies had battled for the Casket and won, then secured it in the Vault so that it might never again be misused.

Thor was furious about the Frost Giants' attack. To him, this was clearly an act of war.

Odin reminded his son that Asgard and Jotunheim had a truce. Who was to say that Laufey ordered this attack? How could Thor know that these Frost Giants were not acting of their own accord? How would Thor have Asgard respond? Odin asked.

Thor replied that he would march to Jotunheim and

teach them a lesson, just as Odin had once done.

Odin fiercely forbid it. No Asgardian would travel to Jotunheim and jeopardize the peace that both Realms had recently enjoyed.

Thor was enraged. His nostrils flared—along with his famous temper. He shouted, overturned banquet tables in the now-empty hall, and smashed anything in his way.

His friends had seen him like this before—it was not atypical behavior for him. Thor grabbed his fabled hammer, Mjolnir, which was cast from the heart of a dying star. He studied the incredibly powerful weapon and told his friends and his brother, Loki, that they were going to Jotunheim.

His friends pleaded with him. Of all the laws of Asgard, this was the one he must not break.

But Thor's mind had been made up. He asked for his friends' trust. This was something they must do.

The Warriors Three and Lady Sif reluctantly agreed, and Loki joined them. As they headed out toward the Bifost, they feared they would live to regret this action and trembled at the thought of Odin's rage coming down upon them.

All of them quaked with fright, except for Thor: Thor the mighty. Thor the arrogant. Thor the foolish.

CHAPTER EIGHT

TONY TOOK THE ELEVATOR to this penthouse apartment and punched in his security code.

"J.A.R.V.I.S.?"

"Welcome home, sir."

Strange. J.A.R.V.I.S. didn't turn on the lights for Tony upon his arrival, as he normally would. Tony knew something was wrong.

"I am Iron Man," a flat and sardonic voice came from the shadows on the far side of the room. "You think you're the only Super Hero in the world? Mr. Stark, you've become part of a bigger universe. You just don't know it yet."

Tony noticed the shadows shifting near the area where the voice was coming from. He balled his fists and readied himself for a fight.

"And exactly who are you?" Tony asked as the figure moved closer.

"Nick Fury, director of S.H.I.E.L.D.," the voice said as its owner stepped out of the shadows. He was a tall, formidable looking man, who wore a patch over his left eye—an eye that was scarred by what looked like the claws of a ferocious animal.

"Huh . . ." Tony said, still on guard.

"I'm here to talk to you about the Avenger Initiative."

JOTUNHEIM

Five great warriors of Asgard traversed the frozen landscape of Jotunheim. Thor led them toward Laufey, king of the Realm's Frost Giants. The son of Odin was determined, filled with a euphoria he only experienced on adventures such as these.

The party accompanying Thor was not quite as thrilled with the experience. Most did not agree with Thor's decision to defy Odin's orders, but joined him because they were loyal friends. As they trudged over the ice-covered soil of Jotunheim, they learned that even the fiercest warriors of Asgard could fall prey to a chill so painful as to burrow into their bones and make it seem as though their limbs might snap from their bodies.

The warriors knew nothing of their course. They anticipated the battle would come to them once the Frost Giants discerned that Asgardians had entered Jotunheim. From what they could observe through a blizzard, they were journeying through an endless, barren landscape of ice. Not a soul was to be seen.

But then the giants began to emerge, seemingly from the landscape itself. They surrounded the Asgardians and squinted their glowing amber eyes as they asked what business they had in Jotunheim. Thor raised his head arrogantly and told them he would speak only to their king. And with that, Laufey, king of Jotunheim, appeared. His skin was a pale blue, like that of the other Frost Giants, but he towered over even the other Jotuns.

Thor asked Laufey how it was that Frost Giants came to enter Asgard. Laufey replied that Odin's house was full of traitors. This disparaging comment angered Thor, and he threateningly raised Mjolnir. Loki urged his brother to calm down. They were outnumbered. They should return home.

The Frost Giants extended their arms, which became encased in swordlike shapes of rock-hard ice. The Asgardians rallied around Thor, readying their own weapons.

For a moment time became still, palpable. And then a brutal battle erupted between the two parties. Ice splintered and shattered as it was smashed by Asgardian and Jotun weaponry. As the battle continued, it also escalated. The scene was more horrible than any battlefield on which the warriors had ever fought before. It seemed that nothing would end this confrontation save the totally annihilation of every living being fighting in it.

And then, the sky became charged with energy, as Odin rode his eight-legged horse, Sleipnir, down from the telltale Bifrost portal onto Jotunheim. He was fitted in golden battle gear and carried his all-powerful staff, Gungnir. He urged Laufey to join him in condemning the battle, but Laufey refused. All of Odin's efforts—his wise leadership, his diplomacy—had been in vain. The truce he'd worked so hard to secure was broken. And his son, Thor, next in line for the throne of Asgard, was to blame.

Odin slammed his staff on the ground, sending the Frost Giants toppling. At the same time, he commanded the Asgardians back over the Bifrost and home to Asgard.

CHAPTER NINE

HIGH ABOVE THE SEA in his cliff-side Malibu residence with beautiful views, Tony was sparring with his pal and chauffer, Hogan. Though at the current time, Hogan was feeling more like a punching bag than a pal.

"What the heck was that?" he barked at Tony, who had just walloped him upside the head.

"It's called mixed martial arts. It's been around for three . . . weeks . . . now."

"It's *called* 'dirty boxing', and there's nothing *new* about it!" Hogan replied.

Before Hogan could throw another punch, a stunningly beautiful woman with deep red hair and dressed in business attire entered the room with a portfolio. She glanced expressionless toward Tony and Hogan and strode over to Pepper, opening the portfolio and presenting her with the papers inside.

"I promise you this is the only time I will ask you to sign over your company," Pepper said to Tony as she began to sign the papers. She loved teasing him now that Tony had decided to put her in charge of Stark Industries. He figured he had enough on his plate to begin with, and had to face the fact that Pepper had sort of been running the place all along.

"I need you to initial each box and sign on the *X*'s," the woman told Pepper.

As Pepper signed, the woman looked over toward Tony and Hogan's exercise. Tony clearly had the upper hand due to his amazing flexibility and natural agility.

Tony noticed the woman staring. Never shy, Tony pointed at her.

"What's your name, lady?"

"Rushman. Natalie Rushman," she responded.

"Front and center, enter the church," Tony said, inviting her into the ring.

"No, you're not going to . . ." Pepper protested.

"It's fine," Natalie said, as she folded the portfolio neatly and carried it with her to the ring.

"I'm sorry . . . he's just . . . very . . . eccentric . . ." Pepper said.

Tony lifted the ring's ropes and Natalie stepped in. The two stared at each other for an awkward, silent moment. Then Tony turned to Hogan and asked him to give her a lesson.

With Natalie otherwise occupied, Tony left the ring and sat down next to Pepper.

"Who is she?" he asked Pepper.

"She is from legal."

"I need an assistant, boss."

"Yes, I have three excellent candidates lined up for you."

"I don't have time to meet them," Tony said, wiping sweat from his brow. "I need someone now. I feel like it's her."

"No it's not," Pepper replied.

While Tony executed a web search on Ms. Rushman and argued the many reasons she was qualified to be his assistant, an unexpected crash sounded from the direction of the ring.

Tony and Pepper looked up. Natalie had flipped Hogan down, rolled on top of him, twisted her legs into a position that looked nearly physically impossible, and pinned him to the ring in a powerful leg-lock.

Pepper screamed and Tony yelped, rushing over to the ring.

"I . . . just, uh, slipped," Hogan said to cover for himself as Natalie slid out of the ring.

"I need your impression," Natalie told Tony.

"Quiet reserve, I don't know, you have an old soul . . ."

"I *meant* your fingerprint. . . ."

"Right."

She handed Tony the forms that Pepper had signed and Tony pressed his finger down to seal the deal. He turned to Pepper.

"You're the boss," he said.

"Will that be all, Mr. Stark?" Natalie asked.

"Yes, that will be all, Ms. Rushman. Thank you very much," Pepper answered for her former boss—who was now her employee. Then she smiled at Tony as he watched Natalie walk gracefully from the room.

ASGARD

Odin could not contain his anger at his son. The Allfather was enraged. He told Thor that he was a vain, greedy, cruel boy. Thor retorted that his father was an old man and a fool. Odin agreed that he had been a fool—to think Thor was ready for the throne of Asgard. He told Thor that he was unworthy of the Realm of Asgard, unworthy of his title. Odin stripped Thor of his armor, his title, and his hammer, all of which would be returned to Thor if he proved himself worthy.

And then Odin, in all his rage *screamed,* "In the name of my father and of his father before, I cast you out!" *He then uttered an incantation that would forever change not only his son, but Asgard and Midgard as well:* "Whosoever holds this hammer, if he be worthy, shall possess the power of Thor."

CHAPTER TEN

TONY WAS TIRED and weary. Ever since his first mission in Afghanistan, the government had been on his case about the Iron Man suit. They felt strongly it should be theirs, not Tony's, to own. It all culminated in a party-gone-bad the night before, when Rhodey had taken one of the Iron Man suits to deliver it to the military. This was, of course, against Tony's wishes, and the whole thing had turned into pretty big mess, especially when Rhodey put on the armor and battled Tony—who was wearing his. Two Iron Men blasting each other with repulsors did not a pleasant scene make!

To make matters worse, Tony had received a call from Colonel Fury saying he'd like to meet with him. Tony, still wearing his Iron Man suit from the night before, chose a place as good as any other: while Tony was waiting, he decided to spend his time the best way possible—enjoying a box of freshly baked doughnuts on top of a doughnut shop, reclining comfortably inside the huge hole of the tremendous plaster doughnut that sat on the roof.

"Sir," Fury called out to him, "I'm going to have to ask you to exit the doughnut."

Tony sighed, then rocketed down and entered through the back door, meeting Fury at his table.

"I told you, I don't want to join your supersecret boy band," Tony said.

Fury laughed condescendingly.

"No, no, no. You see, I remember—you do everything yourself. . . . How's that working out for you?"

"It's, it's . . . I'm sorry, I don't want to get off on the wrong foot. Do I look you in the patch, or the eye?"

Fury didn't entertain Tony with a response.

"Honestly, I'm really tired, and I'm not sure if you're real, if you're just some sort of a . . ."

"I. Am. Very. Real," Fury said. "I'm the realest person you're ever going to meet."

"Just my luck. Where's the staff here?"

A woman strode up to the table, but she wasn't a waitress.

"We've secured the perimeter, but I don't think we can hold it too much longer."

Tony was stunned, which did not happen often. The woman who had approached them was a S.H.I.E.L.D. agent. But she was also Stark's legal counsel—Natalie Rushman.

Colonel Fury smiled, enjoying the shock on Tony's face and relishing in seeing him speechless for once.

"Huh," Tony said after examining Natalie. "You're fired."

"That's not up to you," she said, taking a seat at the table along with Fury and Tony.

"Tony," Colonel Fury said, "I want you to meet Agent Natasha Romanoff."

"Hi," Tony said, with mock enthusiasm.

"I'm a S.H.I.E.L.D. shadow. I was tasked to you by Director Fury," Natalie—or, rather, Natasha—explained.

"I suggest you apologize," Tony said.

Natasha just sneered in response.

"You've been very busy," Fury piped up. "You made your girl your CEO; you're giving away all your stuff; you let your friend fly off with your suit. Now, if I didn't know better . . ."

"You *don't* know better," Tony protested. "I didn't give it to him, he took it."

"Whoa, whoa, whoa. What? No. He *took* it? You're *Iron Man*, and he just *took* it?" Fury said. "Is that possible?" he asked, turning to Agent Romanoff.

"Well, according to Mr. Stark's database-security guidelines, there are redundancies to prevent unauthorized usage," Natasha reported.

Fury shrugged at Tony, indicating that he had some explaining to do.

"What do you want from me? Tony asked.

"What do we want from you? Nuh-uh-uh," Fury said. "What do *you* want from *me*? *You* have become a problem, a problem *I* have to deal with."

Tony had tried a few times to get a word in edgewise. But he eventually gave up. Fury would always have the last one.

"Contrary to your belief, you are *not* the center of my universe," Fury continued his tirade. "I've got bigger problems than you in the Southwest region to deal with."

CHAPTER ELEVEN

THE GOD OF THUNDER, son of Odin, was propelled through space and time to a dark and rocky landscape worlds away from his home in both grandeur and dimension. As he rocketed to Midgard—to *Earth*—he saw ahead of him the dim lights of a motorized vehicle, the likes of which was unfamiliar to him. Disoriented from his journey, there was no way to prevent a collision. He was soon hit hard and laid out on the dusty ground.

Erik Selvig, who had been a passenger, sprung out, along with the driver, Jane Foster, and Darcy Lewis, who assisted them. Jane rushed to Thor's side.

"Do me a favor and don't be dead," Jane said as Thor breathed heavily, attempting to recover from both the vehicle's impact and his exile to Midgard.

The son of Odin raised himself on his elbows

and stared into Jane's face. She resembled those who lived on Asgard, but there was a look in her eyes that betrayed fear and concern—a look Thor knew was unique to mortals.

Finally, Jane sighed in relief. The man she'd hit didn't look very hurt at all.

"Where did he come from?" she asked her colleagues.

At the same time, Thor regained much of his strength and fully picked himself up. He spun around, attempting to regain his bearings. Where was Mjolnir? He began to call out for his hammer. Then he called out for Heimdall, guardian of the Bifrost. Finally, he began to question the group about the Realm on which he'd landed.

"Ohmygosh," Jane said, examining the sky above the spot where Thor had landed. "Look at this. We need to take a record of it before it all changes."

"Jane, we have to take him to the hospital," Erik replied.

"Oh, he's fine! Look at him," Jane said, motioning to Thor who now appeared to be fully recovered.

"Heimdall! I know you can hear me! Open the Bifrost!" Thor shouted to the sky.

Jane winced. "Right. Hospital. You go. I'll stay."

But before Erik could take Thor anywhere, the mighty son of Odin spun around.

"You," he pointed at Darcy. "What Realm is this? Alfheim? Nornheim?"

"New Mexico . . . ?" Darcy replied. Instinctively, she lifted her Taser toward Thor and trained its red target beam on him.

Thor puffed out his chest.

"You *dare* threaten me, *Thor*, with so *puny* a weapon?"

With that, Darcy pulled her trigger and zapped Thor, who quivered from the electrical pulses that coursed through him before finally collapsing.

Erik and Jane looked at Darcy in disbelief.

"What?" she asked. "He was freaking me out!"

The three struggled to lift Thor, whose weight was considerable.

"Darcy, next time you Taser somebody, make sure he's already in the car, okay?" Erik said.

Before long, the three had arrived at the hospital. As the medics took Thor to the ER, Jane, Darcy, and Erik registered him.

"Name?" the receptionist requested.

"He said it was . . . Thor?" Jane responded, skeptically.

"And your relationship to him?"

"I've never met him before"

"Until she hit him with a car," Darcy added.

"I *grazed* him," Jane interjected, "but *she* Tasered him."

"Yes, I did," Darcy proudly admitted.

Shouts and commotion were then heard in the direction of Thor's examining room.

"How dare you attack the son of Odin?"

Glass was breaking, metal was clanging, and medical instruments could be heard crashing to the ground. Thor made his way out of the examining room and toward reception, followed by a great number of hospital workers. Two workers were able to steady Thor and push him up against a wall.

"You are no match for the Mighty . . ."

But before Thor could finish his sentence, he was pricked in the back with a needle and collapsed to the ground.

CHAPTER TWELVE

AGENT COULSON pulled up to on the side of a desert cliff and parked his car near the edge. He stepped up to the rocky ledge and looked out over the desert. Before him was a huge crater, similar to the kind a dangerously sized meteor might cause. The crater was filled with people drinking, laughing, partying, and lining up around an object at the center of the impact.

He removed his sunglasses to get a better look. Then he took out his smart phone and called Director Fury.

"Sir, we found it," he said.

Meanwhile, back at Jane's makeshift lab, which was set up in a former automobile dealership in the small New Mexican town of Puente Antiguo, Erik, Jane, and Darcy were examining the data that Jane had collected the night they'd met Thor.

"What do you see?" she asked Erik.

"Stars," Erik replied.

"Yeah, but not *our* stars."

She held up a celestial map. "See? *This* is the star alignment for our quadrant this time of year. And unless Ursa Minor decided to take a day off, these are someone else's constellations."

"Hey, check this out!" Darcy called from across the room.

Jane and Erik ran over to another wall of photos. In one of the pictures, the unmistakable figure of a man could be seen spinning amid the swirl of electrical clouds.

"No, it can't be!" Erik said.

"I think I left something at the hospital," Jane said, and then she quickly left the lab, with Erik and Darcy trailing not far behind.

They soon arrived at the hospital, but when they got there they discovered Thor had broken out without their help—trashing the place in the process.

"We just lost our most important piece of evidence. Typical!" Jane said.

"Now what?" asked Darcy.

"We find him," Jane said.

"Did you see what he did in there?" asked Erik. "I'm not sure if finding him is the best idea."

"Well, our data can't tell us what it was like to be inside that event, and he can. So, we're going to find him."

As Jane backed her car out of its parking spot, she slammed into something big, solid, and blond. She put her truck in park, threw open the door, and jumped out. She rushed to Thor's side.

"I'm so sorry! I swear I'm not doing this on purpose!"

Apology accepted, Thor expressed how hungry he was.

"This mortal form is weak," he said. "I need sustenance."

They ducked into a diner and continued their conversation there.

"How did you get inside that cloud?" Jane asked as Thor polished off an entire box of breakfast pastries, followed by a plate of pancakes, then two orders of eggs and another of waffles. He'd also discovered a taste for coffee.

"This drink . . ." he said. "I like it. Another!" he shouted, smashing the mug on the floor.

Jane apologized to the staff, scurrying to clean up the mess.

"What was that?" she asked.

"It was delicious, I want another."

"Well, you could have just said that."

"I just did!"

"I mean, asked nicely."

"I meant no disrespect."

"All right, well, no more smashing, deal?"

Thor agreed begrudgingly. "You have my word."

Just then, a group of men walked in and sat at the counter. They were talking about a satellite that had crashed in the desert. They said it looked "like a hammer or something." Nobody could lift it. People had a lot of fun trying though—until federal agents stepped in and secured the area.

Overhearing this, Thor stepped over to the men at the counter.

"Which way?" he asked

"Fifty miles west of here," one responded. "But I wouldn't waste my time. It looked like the whole army was coming when we left."

Thor rushed out of the diner, and Jane, Erik, and Darcy followed him.

"Where are you going?" Jane asked.

"Fifty miles west of here."

"Why?"

"To get what belongs to me."

"Oh, so you own a satellite now?"

"It's not what they say it is."

"Well, whatever it is, the government seems to think it's theirs—so, you just intend to go in there and take it?"

"Yes." Thor smiled, and with that he was off.

CHAPTER THIRTEEN

WHILE THOR WAS journeying to retrieve Mjolnir, Jane, Erik, and Darcy, were returning to the lab. But when they arrived, they were thrown by the scene there—Coulson and a number of other S.H.I.E.L.D. agents had identified the lab as a wellspring of data pertaining to the event, and they were removing all of its contents.

"What is going on here?" Jane said, as she rushed in.

"Ms. Foster, I'm Agent Coulson with S.H.I.E.L.D."

"Is that supposed to *mean* something to me? You can't do this!"

"Jane," Erik said, pulling her aside. "Jane, this is a lot more serious than you realize. Let it go."

"Let it go? This is my *life*."

"We're investigating a security threat," Agent Coulson explained. "We need to appropriate your records and all your atmospheric data."

"By 'appropriate' do you mean 'steal'?"

Jane walked over to a S.H.I.E.L.D. van, into which the agents were loading all of her equipment. Agent Coulson followed close behind her.

"Here," he said, handing her a check. "This should more than compensate you for your trouble."

"I can't just *buy* replacements! I made most of this equipment myself!" Jane pleaded.

"Then I'm sure you can do it again," Coulson retorted.

"And I'm sure I can sue you for violating my constitutional rights!"

"I'm sorry, Ms. Foster, but we're the good guys."

"So are *we*," Jane said passionately. "I'm on the verge of understanding something extraordinary, and everything I know about this phenomenon is either in this lab or in this book in my hand, and you can't just take it away. . . ."

Before Jane could complete her thought, another S.H.I.E.L.D. agent stepped up from behind and grabbed the journal from her hand.

"Hey!" Jane protested.

With that, the S.H.I.E.L.D. agents brushed Jane aside and locked her research in their van.

"Thank you for your cooperation," said Agent Coulson. Then he jumped in the van and drove off.

"Who are these people?" Jane asked as the van pulled away.

"I knew this scientist—a pioneer in gamma radiation. S.H.I.E.L.D. showed up and—well—he wasn't heard from again."

Jane looked stunned for a moment, then defiantly declared, "They're not going to do that to us. I'm going to get everything back."

"Come on, please," Erik said. "Let me contact one of my colleagues. He's had some dealings with these people before. I'll e-mail him, and maybe he can help. . . ."

"They took *your* laptop, too," Darcy reminded him.

Jane had other, more practical solutions. She was going to find Thor, and they'd travel to the site together. He would help her retrieve her data. And, if he really was who he said he was and not some crazy lunatic, she'd help him get back what he was looking for.

She drove around the town until she found him— which wasn't too difficult given his height and heft.

"Still need a lift?" she asked him.

Thor hopped in without hesitation.

By the time they arrived at the site, night had fallen. Jane pulled up to a dark area at the rim of the crater, and she and Thor jumped out of the truck and looked down at the scene. S.H.I.E.L.D. had built an incredibly elaborate structure within the crater's pit. It was brightly lit, with high-tech tubing creating passageways to and from the center, which was sectioned off in a huge glass-walled cube.

"That's no satellite crash," Jane observed. "They would have hauled the wreckage away. They wouldn't have built a city around it."

"You're going to need this," Thor said, wrapping a jacket around Jane.

"Huh? Wait, why?"

Thor smiled broadly and laughed.

"Stay here," he said. "Once I have Mjolnir, I will return the items they stole from you."

"Look what's down there. You think you're just going to walk in, grab our stuff, and walk out?"

"No. I'm going to fly out."

The Tesseract was guarded by Hawkeye at a secret
S.H.I.E.L.D. base.

Loki found a way into the heavily-guarded S.H.I.E.L.D. base
and stole the Tesseract!

S.H.I.E.L.D. contacted Tony Stark about the Avengers
Initiative, but Tony wasn't interested in joining the team.

Then Fury sent Black Widow to Calcutta to find scientist
Bruce Banner.

Fury also went to the last person to encounter the Tesseract—Captain America.

The heroes soon assembled on the Helicarrier for their mission to retrieve the Tesseract and stop Loki.

To battle against an Asgardian, Steve Rogers would need a new-and-improved Captain America combat suit.

The heroes found Loki in Germany, and the First Avenger led the charge!

Just when Loki thought he had the upper hand, Iron Man flew in to save the day.

Working together, Iron Man and Cap stopped Loki . . . but someone mightier had plans for the Trickster.

Thor took his brother from the heroes so that Loki could face Asgardian justice.

Earth's Mightiest Heroes battled amongst themselves to retrieve the Tesseract and stop Loki from escaping.

Thor, Cap, and Iron Man finally worked as a team to defeat Loki and locate the Tesseract.

But Loki knew that the cell he was in was originally meant for someone bigger and greener.

Now, whenever there is a threat too big for any one hero to handle, the Mighty Avengers assemble to protect the Earth!

And with that, Thor headed toward the encampment.

As he approached Mjolnir, clouds rolled in and lightning flashed all over the area, interfering with S.H.I.E.L.D.'s equipment. Thor took advantage of this, and sneaked past some guards, easily taking out those that he could not get by. Slipping in and out of shadows, Thor made his way toward his hammer. The lightning and thunder intensified. Soon, rain poured down on the site, muddying the desert sands and pounding on everyone from Thor to Jane, who finally understood why Thor had given her the coat.

Thor soon arrived near Mjolnir, which was heavily guarded. S.H.I.E.L.D. had its top agents keeping watch over the hammer, including its ace archer, Clint Barton, whose aim was so accurate he'd earned the codename Hawkeye. Clint was trained on Thor and waiting for orders to shoot, but Coulson—who was calling the shots—asked him to hold off. He wanted to see if Thor could lift the hammer.

Thor looked down at his old friend, Mjolnir. He smiled and reached down in triumph. He and his hammer were reunited. He would now reclaim it and then get Jane's data back. He reached down and gripped Mjolnir by the handle, enjoying the comfort of its familiar grip.

But when he moved to raise it, the hammer would not relent. It proved immovable. Thor looked up at the heavens and howled up at Odin, the Bifrost, and all of Asgard. He dropped to his knees in defeat. Agent Barton dropped his bow, and S.H.I.E.L.D. agents moved in to detain the god of thunder.

MIDGARD

Unbeknownst to Heimdall, the sentry who guarded the Bifrost, Loki traveled to Midgard, where his brother was banished. Loki had learned that he was adopted, but decided not to share that information until the time was right. Instead, the adopted brother of the Mighty Thor would speak to his sibling, who was in captivity on Midgard.

Their father—Odin—was dead, Loki told Thor, lying. Thor's banishment, the threat of a new war—these things were too much for him to bear. Odin had perished from the loss and disappointment, and the burden of the Asgardian throne had now fallen to Loki.

Thor, stunned and stricken with grief, asked if he could return home, and Loki spun more lies.

The truce with Jotunheim was conditional upon Thor's exile, Loki told his brother. Frigga, Thor's mother, had forbidden her son's return, Loki said, completing his deceitful tale.

With that, Loki bade his brother good-bye with a word of condolence.

Thor, with a heavy heart, said that he was the one who was sorry. He thanked his brother for coming to him to deliver the message, and, with a final farewell, the vision of Loki was gone.

CHAPTER FOURTEEN

FROM THE OUTSIDE, it looked like an abandoned factory tucked away amid vacant lots beneath a Los Angeles freeway. Two town cars and an unbelievably slick sports car were parked in the shadows, well hidden from any wandering eyes that might find their way to the space. Long-defunct railroad tracks surrounded it, and puddles of oil marred the cracked concrete.

Inside sat one of the world's richest and smartest men. He was seated at a table, facing an empty chair and surrounded by fantastically high-tech screens. One was lit up with the S.H.I.E.L.D. insignia. Another kept track of current news events with a constant feed of international newscasts. Still another showed stock quotes, weather reports from around the world, and hotspots of what could only be classified as strange activity.

After a few minutes of perusing the various displays, Tony grew bored and turned his attention to the desk. On it was a small stack of printed files. Curious, Tony grabbed the top one and checked out the cover, which read: AVENGERS INITIATIVE: PRELIMINARY REPORT

Intrigued, Tony opened it up to take a look.

But before he could digest any information, a powerful hand swept down and grabbed the folder from him. Tony looked up into the familiar face of Colonel Nick Fury. Although Tony repeatedly said he didn't want any part of the Avengers Initiative, there was something about it that interested him, so he kept coming back.

"I don't think I want you looking at that," Fury said as he sat down at the table. "I'm not sure it pertains to you anymore."

Colonel Fury held up a similar file. "Now *this* on the other hand, is Agent Romanoff's assessment of *you*. Read it."

He tossed the file to Tony, who opened it and began to read.

"Aaaaaaaaah . . . *Personality overview: Mister Stark displays* compulsive behavior.' . . . In my own defense, that *was* last week."

Colonel Fury shot Tony a warning glance.

"'*Prone to self-destructive tendencies . . .*' I mean, please. And aren't we all?"

The colonel kept Tony locked under his stern gaze.

"'*Textbook . . . narcissism*'? . . . Agreed."

Despite the fact that Fury's expression had not changed at all, his anger was becoming more and more palpable.

"Okay, here it is . . . '*Recruitment Assessment for Avenger Initiative—Iron Man: Yes.*'"

Tony flung the file back at Fury, gloating.

"I've got to think about it."

"Read on," Fury replied flatly.

Tony again picked up the file. "'*Tony Stark: Not . . .* **Not**? *. . . Recommended*'?"

Colonel Fury leaned back in his chair and raised an eyebrow at Tony.

"That doesn't make any sense," Tony protested. "How can you approve *me*, but not approve me? I've got a new ticker; I'm trying to do right by Pepper; I'm in a stable-ish relationship . . ."

"Which leads us to believe that at this juncture we'd only like to use you as a consultant," Fury explained.

Tony looked a little bit bummed. He nodded, then stood up and extended his hand to Fury. Fury took it, and as they shook Tony smiled and said to him, "You can't afford me."

CHAPTER FIFTEEN

AGENT COULSON WAS hard at work dealing with the situation in New Mexico. He had spent the previous night interrogating the powerful man who had broken into the complex where the hammer that had fallen to Earth was being held. Coulson had pressed him on where he came from and how it was that he found himself in a S.H.I.E.L.D. facility. The man was clearly highly trained, and Coulson wanted to know where he received that training. Pakistan? Chechnya? Afghanistan?

The man remained silent. Coulson was going to find out who this mercenary was and what he wanted. He spent the whole night trying, though, and had gotten nothing.

Now, he'd received a call that someone had arrived with information.

* * *

"His name's Donald Blake?" Coulson asked skeptically, as he met Dr. Selvig at the heavily armed entrance to the site.

"*Dr.* Donald Blake," Selvig replied.

"You have dangerous coworkers, Dr. Selvig."

"He was destroyed when he found out you'd taken all of our research. That was years of his life. Gone. I can understand how a man might go off like that. The big face of an organization like yours coming in with jack-booted thugs . . . Well, that's how he put it anyway."

"That still doesn't explain how he managed to tear through our security."

"Steroids!" Erik lied, but he said it as if it were the most obvious explanation in the world.

After engaging Dr. Coulson some more, Dr. Selvig was allowed in to collect the detainee.

"Donnie, Donnie, Donnie, there you are. Gonna be all right. I'm taking you home now!"

Thor and Erik walked silently from the camp. As they departed, Thor managed to swipe Jane's notebook from an agent, completely unnoticed.

It seemed they were free and clear.

CHAPTER SIXTEEN

THE FOLLOWING morning, Thor received a visit from four heavily armored friends who erased any lingering doubt in Erik's, Jane's, and Darcy's minds that Thor truly was from Asgard. Thor's closest companions, Lady Sif and the Warriors Three—Hogun, Volstagg, and Fandral—had arrived via the Bifrost. Their spectacular Asgardian battle armor attracted the notice of everyone in the town, including a duo of S.H.I.E.L.D. agents that Coulson had sent to shadow Thor and Selvig after he let Thor go.

Thor embraced his longtime companions, overjoyed to see their familiar, brave faces.

"Oh, my friends!" he shouted. "This is good! This is good! My friends, I have never been happier to see anyone. But you should not have come."

"We have come to take you home," Fandral said.

"You know I can't go home. My father is dead because of me and I must remain in exile."

Lady Sif shook her head. "Thor, your father still lives."

Thor looked stunned.

Before anyone else could respond, a funnel formed in the otherwise-cloudless desert sky, and with it a whipping sandstorm that shook cars and cut anything in its path appeared as if from nowhere—just as Thor had when he first arrived on Earth.

"Was somebody else coming?" Darcy asked, not sure what to make of any of this.

As if on cue, the dust lifted and revealed a huge, otherworldly, humanlike figure covered in metal. It was the Destroyer.

"Is that one of Stark's?" Agent Sitwell asked Coulson.

"I don't know, that guy never tells me anything," Coulson replied.

Coulson stepped up to the twenty-foot being, held up a megaphone to it, and announced, "Hello. You are using unregistered weapons technology. Identify yourself."

In response, the Destroyer revealed its face—a fiery

furnace—and began to shoot energy from it, vaporizing anything it came into contact with.

"Jane, you have to leave," Thor said.

"What are you going to do?" Jane asked.

"I'm staying here," Thor replied.

"Thor's going to fight with us!" Volstagg pronounced.

"My friends, I am just a man. I'll only be in the way, and at worst get one of you killed. But I can help get these people to safety."

"Well, if you're staying, then so am I," Jane said.

Thor helped Jane clear the town, loading people into trucks, helping people find their way in the chaos. And while Thor, Jane, Erik, and Darcy did their part, the four Asgardians faced the Destroyer, which they knew the jealous and bitter Loki had sent to Midgard to vanquish his brother.

But one after another, the Asgardians found it impossible to fend off the Destroyer. While Thor's friends—mortal and immortal—took cover, Thor knew what he must do. As Odin's son, as a prince of Asgard, he must combat the Destroyer.

He spoke to Loki from across the Realms.

"Brother, whatever I have done to wrong you, whatever I have done to lead you to do this, I am truly sorry. But these people are innocent. Taking their lives will gain you nothing."

He stepped up to the Destroyer, whose entire body was blazing beneath its armor.

"So take mine," Thor said, "and end this."

With that, the Destroyer closed its faceplate and turned to walk away. Thor was smiling, comforted that his words had reached his brother. But as it was leaving, the Destroyer backhanded Thor and sent him flying hundreds of yards across the dusty town.

"No!" Jane yelled, running over to him.

Thor heaved, bloody and beaten, not able to withstand the blow without his powers.

"It's over," he said to Jane. "You're safe."

Thor closed his eyes. A mighty hero had fallen. His stunned friends looked on as the Destroyer walked off into the horizon.

At that very moment, fifty miles away, Mjolnir began to rattle, shake, and finally break free from its stone encasement. It shot across the desert and landed right in the hand of Thor. Lightning struck, sending a blast of sand and smoke into the desert sky. When the dust cleared, Thor stood, outfitted in his armor and cape. He had proven himself worthy of Mjolnir by his selfless deeds and actions.

Thor twirled Mjolnir victoriously over his head, whipping up a twister that sucked up the Destroyer. Thor battled it in the heart of the storm, easily defeating the being and sending it crashing to the ground before making his own triumphant return.

Now he needed to journey over the Bifrost and return to Asgard to confront his brother. But before he could move to do so, Agent Coulson approached him.

"Excuse me, Donald?" he said. "I don't think you've been completely honest with us."

"You and I fight for the same cause—the protection of this world," Thor said. "From this day forward, you can count me as your ally. If you return the items you have taken from Jane."

"Stolen," Jane clarified.

"Borrowed," Coulson protested. "Of course you can have your equipment back. You're going to need it to continue your research."

Jane beamed.

Heimdall opened the Bifrost.

"I must return to Asgard," Thor said to Jane. "But I give you my word, I will return for you."

And with that, Thor and his Asgardian companions were sucked into a prismatic portal and away from Earth.

BIFROST

Whilst Thor was banished to Midgard, Loki used his time in Asgard to dominate the Realm. The Bifrost, being the key to travel between Realms and also a powerful force of energy in itself, was an integral part of his plan. Loki approached the Rainbow Bridge, used the Casket of Ancient Winters to freeze Heimdall, and traveled over the prismlike road to Jotunheim.

Once in the enemy kingdom, Loki set out to seek Laufey. Upon finding the Jotun king, Loki disclosed how he had sneaked in the Frost Giants during Thor's coronation and offered Laufey the opportunity to re-enter Asgard—this time to murder Odin, who was in the mystical Odinsleep. Loki would then see to it that the Casket of Ancient Winters be returned to its rightful place in Jotunheim, and Laufey and Loki would part in peace.

Laufey, no fool, agreed to Loki's plan. Soon, Frost Giants were marching into Asgard. As the Jotuns invaded, Laufey approached Odin's bedchamber and, smiling, prepared to kill the Allfather. But just before the deed was about to be done, Loki murdered Laufey. Now he would be hailed as a hero. And with Thor banished to Midgard, he would be the rightful ruler of Asgard!

Before Loki could flee Odin's chamber, in order to complete the final phase of his plan—to destroy Jotunheim in order to cement his place in the annals of Asgardian history as the great savior of his people—he noticed that the other Frost Giants had been driven back. Only one warrior in all of Asgard possessed such power—his brother, Thor. But Thor was exiled to Midgard . . .

Thor confronted his brother, and a fierce battle began. It started in Odin's chambers, and soon the two brothers found themselves fighting inside Heimdell's Observatory. Loki planned to steer all the energy of the Rainbow Bridge toward Jotunheim and destroy the Realm.

Thor flew toward Loki and began to struggle with him again. But Loki did not betray his reputation for quickness and trickery. Thor found the battle complicated and difficult, and eventually he realized that the only way to prevent the full-on destruction of Jotunheim was to destroy the Bifrost. He thought about his adventure on Midgard and all that he'd learned—and learned to love—there. He might never be able to return if the Bifrost was destroyed.

He raised Mjolnir and began to hammer away more and more furiously until dazzling crystal pieces of the bridge drifted into the sea of space surrounding it. As the bridge exploded, the two brothers were blasted off the ruined bridge and dangled on the edge of space. But their father, having emerged from his sleep, grabbed hold of Thor, who in turn held on to Loki. Thor did everything he could to save his brother. But Loki allowed himself to slip from Thor's grasp and fell, screaming, into the void of space.

CHAPTER SEVENTEEN

IT WAS DIFFICULT to make out exactly what was happening in New York City, but a large blur of a figure was moving at great speeds, converging with vehicles, buildings, and the ground, and generally wreaking havoc on 125th Street in Harlem.

The destruction was more widespread than it had been earlier. There was more rubble and smoke everywhere. And now for the first time, a camera fixed itself on the face of the monster causing the chaos.

An ugly blue-gray . . . thing—about fifteen feet tall, judging its height compared to the nearby lampposts—looked like a bulging mass of twisted muscle and overgrown bones. Its hands and legs were enormous—each about the size of a tree trunk—and though its head was small as compared to the rest of it, it had a terrifying reptilianlike quality that made it no less intimidating than the rest of the creature. The spikes that protruded from its spine did nothing to soften the look of this thing.

The creature balled its fists, lifted its head, and let out a vicious growl.

Suddenly, a bright green beam shot out of the sky toward the monster followed by a thunderous impact. What was the government doing—nuking the thing with gamma rays now?

The green flash was not a nuke—or any other kind of missile. It was another big ugly thing. This one was green and had hair, and was in no way as grotesque and distorted as the one tearing up the city.

But the ugly monsters were not fighting together— they were fighting each other. The big green one pummeled the ugly one straight down 125th street, and it left a ditch in the asphalt where it skid. A ticker at the bottom of the screen read: CROWDS DESCRIBE RAMPAGING BEAST AS AN ABOMINATION.

The Abomination grabbed the green beast and threw him into a building, which crumbled around him. The green beast didn't even need a minute to a recover, and burst from the rubble as if from water. It leaped in the air and soared a great distance to land on the Abomination, and the two continued to wrestle.

Now the ticker read: HULK APPEARS TO HAVE UPPER HAND.

The two giants faced each other, hunched in ready stances, prepared to attack. Both lunged at the same time, and they collided in midair. The impact created a disturbance that shattered windows as far as ten blocks away.

The beasts continued to attack each other. Then a helicopter, looking very small compared to the larger-than-life scene unfolding below, began to pelt the Abomination with bullets.

The Abomination jumped on top of a roof, and the copter flew in, attempting to achieve more effective fire at closer range. The Abomination grabbed a ten-foot girder from the roof's water tower. He ripped it out, scattering its rivets on the ground. Then he launched the girder into the air as easily as an ordinary man might throw a spear. It clipped the helicopter's rear rotor, and the aircraft started whirling out of control and spiraling toward Earth.

The Hulk took the opportunity to reengage the

Abomination, and the two continued to battle.

The copter crashed into the ground, and the news cameras caught people escaping. A woman ran out of the chopper—and *toward* the scene of the fight.

The Hulk roared as the woman approached. The Abomination tore from the ground two marble posts connected by a chain, using them as bolas. The woman continued to approach. She seemed to be calling out to the Hulk. She must have been in shock. The Hulk raised his arms, and his veins and muscles bulged and pulsed.

The Hulk smashed his hands into the ground and it opened up, creating a great chasm into which his adversary fell. The Hulk moved toward him, and then finished off the Abomination. The Hulk saw to it that the woman was safe, and then bounded off into the New York City night. The Hulk was gone, and the Abomination had been defeated.

CHAPTER EIGHTEEN

TONY OPENED THE dark restaurant's splintered door, flooding it with the bright afternoon sun. Even from outside, he could smell the reeking barroom. Stale drink, cigar smoke—these were not the kinds of smells Tony was used to surrounding himself with. Though disgusted, he strode in as comfortably as if he were walking into a fundraiser at the Waldorf Astoria. He made his way past chatting couples and drinking buddies, straight to General Ross who sat at the other end of the bar.

"I hate to say I told you so, General," Tony started before General Ross even had a chance to look up at him, "but that Super-Soldier program was put on ice for a reason. I've always felt that hardware was more practical."

"Stark!" General Ross said, finally facing Tony.

"General."

"You always wear such nice suits," General Ross said, alluding to Tony's alter ego, who wore the coolest suit of all.

"Touché," Tony responded. He paused and then continued, "I hear you have an unusual problem."

"*You* should talk," General Ross said again taking a stab at Tony's life as Iron Man.

"You should listen."

General Ross took a long puff of his stinking cigar, and Tony coughed a little. Then his face became deadly serious.

"What if I told you we were putting a team together?" Tony asked the general.

"Who's 'we'?" The general responded.

Tony looked pensive, thoughtful, brooding. Then Tony smirked the way he always did when he knew something others didn't . . . which happened quite often.

CHAPTER NINETEEN

SOMETHING WAS HAPPENING in the Arctic Circle, one of the most inhospitable regions on Earth. Wind whipped up snow and ice so furiously that visibility was reduced to within mere feet. Anyone who could bear to leave their naked eyes open long enough would see only thick sheets of snow and ice blowing before him. The arctic desert beat on the rescue vehicles like a frozen sandstorm. As their bright headlights cut through the thick storm around them, wandering aimlessly through the terrain for a place to land, they hit upon the figure of a man, dressed in Inuit garb and waving a flare to signal the vehicle.

The scouts stepped from the relative warmth of their vehicle into the solid snow.

"Are you the guys from Washington?" the man with the flare asked.

"You get many other visitors out here?" one of the men answered, speaking loudly to be heard over the wail of the wind.

"How long have you been on-site?" His companion asked, straining his voice as well.

"Since this morning. A Russian oil team called it in about eighteen hours ago."

"How come nobody spotted it before?"

"It's really not that surprising, This landscape's changing all the time," the man with the flair said as he motioned to the squalls of snow whipping up and over snow-dunes. "You got any idea what this thing is exactly?"

"I don't know, it's probably a weather balloon," one of the men from Washington replied.

"I don't think so." The guide chuckled. "You know, we don't have the equipment for a job like this."

"How long before we can start craning it out?"

"I don't think you quite understand. . . . You guys are going to need one mighty big crane!"

With that, their guide beamed his flashlight toward a huge ice-covered steel slab jutting out from the frozen landscape, like the head of a mammoth whale breaking the surface of the ocean. It appeared to be the wing of some sort of aircraft, but neither of the men had ever before seen a craft like this. The three men looked up at it in awe, wondering what it could possibly be. The flashlights of a half dozen other workers surveyed the metal, examining it for any clues. One of the agents rushed back to the truck and brought back a device that looked equal parts drill and buzz saw. He called for some of the others to assist him, and soon set it on top of the craft.

He flipped a switch and activated the device. The nozzle began to spin with a steady cadence. A blue stream of bright energy shot from the nozzle and cut right through the craft's hull. The cut steel crashed a great distance below, creating a chasm in what now clearly appeared to be some sort of ship.

The agents quickly attached grapples to the body of the vessel and lowered themselves into the craft. The softly falling snow illuminated by the bluish floodlight glowing above the blue aperture heightened the feeling that the men were traveling a passageway to another world.

"What *is* this?" one of the men asked as the two

scouted the area with their flashlight beams.

The men tried to keep themselves steady as they traversed the craft's ice-covered steel and made their way through an area lit only by their flashlights and whatever dim radiance could make its way through the incision above them.

One of the agents' flashlight beams landed on something covered by a thin veil of ice crystals. It looked like a symbol of some sort—a star, circles. There was something familiar about the patterns, but the agent couldn't determine what exactly. He wiped the ice from the object. Whatever he'd found, it should yield some clues to the ship's purpose.

"Lieutenant!" the agent called.

The other approached quickly from behind.

"What is it?" the agent asked the lieutenant.

The lieutenant stared down in dumbfounded amazement. It was an unmistakable emblem—a bold white star set over blue metal—not just any metal, vibranium. And it was ringed with red and white circles. A shield—one that belonged to a hero that some discounted as a myth, a hoax.

"BASE!" the lieutenant called into his monitor.

"Give me a line to the colonel"

"It's three a.m. for him, sir," the base responded.

"I don't care what time it is," the lieutenant said. "This one's waited long enough."

CHAPTER TWENTY

SINCE HIS BATTLE with the Abomination, Bruce had been moving from town to town and country to country, so as not to be tracked down. He knew that S.H.I.E.L.D. was looking for him. He also knew Ross wanted to capture him, force the Hulk out, then dissect it to study and replicate it. But Bruce was the only one who understood just how dangerous and unpredictable the Hulk's power was. He'd been living with it inside him for years now and had spent most of his time finding ways to keep the Hulk locked up. For long stretches, he'd been successful. But on the occasions when someone had been able to track him down, things went terribly wrong.

Bruce was becoming encouraged by the fact that he'd finally gotten the Hulk under some sort control and that he could bring some of himself into the Hulk. He did this when he protected Betty and General Ross from the Abomination, and even when he attacked the Abomination itself—he knew what he was doing, knew what was at stake. And for all the injuries the Hulk caused—and Bruce felt partly responsible for each and every one of them—he'd saved scores of other people who might have perished if the Abomination hadn't been stopped.

What Bruce did not feel great about was S.H.I.E.L.D.'s understanding of what the Hulk was. As he tried to explain on so many occasions, the Hulk was not the kind of thing that could ever be captured, controlled, or studied. S.H.I.E.L.D. seemed to disagree. Keeping himself out of their hands not only protected Bruce himself, but also anyone who would get in the Hulk's way once he'd become enraged.

As a result, he returned to his wandering ways, just as he'd done years ago when he was hiding out in Brazil, where he worked in a bottling plant, or squatting in Mexico as a beggar. Whenever he could do so, he helped whoever needed it along the way. He currently found himself in Calcutta. Bruce had made a life for himself here, and there was really no end to the number of people in need. This kept Bruce in the city longer than most places.

CHAPTER TWENTY-ONE

STEVE ROGERS WOKE in unfamiliar sur-
roundings. He felt refreshed. His head was clear and
he was full of energy, but he couldn't figure out where
he was or how he'd gotten here.

The institutional-looking room was spare. The
steel-frame cot that Steve slept on looked like government issue. The mint-green walls were bare. At the far
corner of the room, a radio played a baseball game. The
Brooklyn Dodgers. Something was wrong.

Steve looked over toward the window from his bed.
The sun was shining and a pleasant breeze was blowing in. By the angle of the sunlight it appeared to be
late morning.

Judging by the soaring brick towers, he could tell
he was in Manhattan. He was dressed in a T-shirt
emblazoned with the insignia of the SSR—the Special

Scientific Reserve organization that had given him strength and agility that were the pinnacle of human potential.

Steve again considered the game on the radio. The Dodgers had scored another three runs. Yes, something was very wrong.

The steel knob of the only door in the room turned, and a pretty nurse walked into Steve's quarters.

"Good morning," she said. "Or should I say afternoon?"

"Where am I?" Steve asked.

"You're in a recovery room in New York City."

"Where am I, really?" Steve asked again, more emphatic this time.

"I'm afraid I don't understand," the nurse said, smiling.

"The game. It's from May 1941. I know because I was there. Now I'm going to ask you again—where am I?"

"Captain Rogers . . ." the nurse tried to explain.

"Who are you?" Steve shouted.

Steve noticed the nurse click a device concealed in her hand. He sprang up and used all his power to smash through a far wall. The illusion of the room fell away as Steve stepped into what looked like the back-stage area of the movie sets he knew from recording newsreel footage.

"Backstage," Steve realized that the images of New York skyscrapers and the late morning sky were simply extremely high-tech projections. He rushed out of the strange room and found himself outside of the building in an alien world that seemed something like the one he'd known, but unbelievably different at the same time.

An imposing man in a long trench coat stepped forward. He wore a patch over his left eye.

"At ease, soldier," the man called out. "Look, I'm sorry about that little show back there, but we thought it best to break it to you slowly."

"Break *what*?" Steve asked.

"You've been asleep, Cap. For almost seventy years."

Steve was speechless. To the passersby in Times Square this was all ordinary.

But to Steve, this was the future.

CHAPTER TWENTY-TWO

DR. ERIK SELVIG found himself in a dimly lit corridor at a S.H.I.E.L.D. research compound. Not long ago he was just a scientist, and now he suddenly found himself in the middle of cross-dimensional superheroic struggles.

"Dr. Selvig," came a voice at the end of the hall.

Selvig turned to see Colonel Fury.

"So, you're the man behind all of this?" Selvig asked. "It's quite a labyrinth. I was thinking you were taking me down here to kill me." He laughed uncomfortably.

Fury did not return his laughter, paused, and then walked toward the doctor.

"I've been hearing about the New Mexico situation. Your work has impressed a lot of people who are much smarter than I am," Fury said.

"I have a lot to work with. A gateway to another dimension—it's unprecedented."

Fury looked Selvig in the eye.

"Isn't it?" Selvig asked.

Fury continued down the hall, with Selvig in tow.

"Legend tells us one thing, history another," Fury said. "But every now and then we find something that belongs to both."

He opened a secure box. Inside was illuminated red circuitry, a security keypad and, in the center, an unusual glittering blue cube, smoother and shinier than anything Selvig had ever seen before. It crackled with electricity, and forks of charged current danced around it.

"What is it?" Selvig asked.

"Power, doctor," Fury replied. "If we can figure out how to tap it, maybe *unlimited* power."

Selvig stared at the cube in awe. But unseen by Fury or Selvig, the spirit of something else looked on—something far more powerful than either of them. Something from another world—a prince of lies, a power-hungry god: Loki.

"Well, I guess that's worth a look . . ." Loki hissed,

grinning, unheard by the mortals surrounding him.

"Well, I guess that's worth a look," Selvig repeated, not realizing the words were not his own—that he was simply captivated by Loki's spell.

Loki was pleased. Thor and Odin thought him dead. He'd tricked them when he fell from the Bifrost. They would not be interfering with his plan. He'd find a way to send himself, body and soul, back to Midgard, and once he was there, he would rule these simple mortals, in a way he wasn't able to rule Asgard.

A Realm would be his at last—just as he deserved.

CHAPTER TWENTY-THREE

IN DR. SELVIG'S research, he uncovered the storied history of the cube—or the Tesseract, as it was officially known. It was once the jewel of Odin's treasure room. The details of how it came to Earth were unclear, but it surely happened when Asgardians traveled over the Bifrost. Ultimately, the Tesseract came to be guarded by a secret society in Tonsberg, Norway. But in March 1942, it was stolen by Johann Schmidt and used as a weapon against HYDRA's enemies—including Captain America. During the Captain's struggle with the Red Skull aboard the HYDRA Valkyrie aircraft—a battle that sent Cap into a frozen deep sleep—the Tesseract was activated, burned through the hull, and plummeted to Earth, where it was buried near the crash site and later retrieved by S.H.I.E.L.D. They knew that, like Thor's hammer, the Tesseract needed to be guarded by their best agent, and so they put Barton on duty overseeing it.

Doctor Selvig found the cube amazing. The way light and matter and energy reacted around it was like nothing he had ever seen. But not long into Dr. Selvig's study of the Tesseract, it began to act oddly, even for a mystical object.

Upon learning from Dr. Selvig that the cube had activated itself, so to speak, Colonel Fury called an emergency meeting with Agents Coulson and Maria Hill. Dr. Selvig told the group that the cube was pulling energy from space and emitting low levels of gamma radiation.

In describing the way in which energy was flowing from—or rather *into* the cube—Agent Hill expressed the very real concern that it could be pulling enough dark energy toward it to collapse all matter on Earth and create a black hole.

"Dr. Selvig," Fury said, "I need a report on the Tesseract."

"She's been misbehaving," Selvig said, never taking his eyes from the cube.

"Where's Barton?" Fury asked.

"The Hawk is in his nest," Selvig replied.

* * *

"I thought I told you to stay close, Agent," Fury shouted up to Barton, who was watching the cube from a crow's nest above.

"My eyesight is better from up here," Barton replied.

"Well, if that's the case, have you seen anything or anyone come or go that might be causing it to act this way?"

Agent Barton rappelled down to speak to Fury face-to-face, and responded in the negative. As Barton understood it, the Tesseract was a doorway to the other end of space. "If there's tampering going on," he said, "it's not from our side of the doorway, but the other one."

Suddenly the cube began to spin, slowly at first, and then faster and faster. It began to glow brighter until it seemed to tear a hole in the very air, revealing stars and celestial dust within.

"Oh, my . . ." Dr. Selvig began.

A man clawed his way through this portal, clutching a staff. He was crouched and shaking—his face regal but gaunt and fatigued, clearly weary from his journey. Still, without delay, he lifted his staff and began to use it to blast violent streams of energy at the agents in the room.

Fury yelled to protect the Tesseract, and the agents, led by Agent Barton, rushed it to safety.

The being who had just entered the room looked up wearily. Mustering as much strength as he could, he touched his staff to Selvig's heart, then turned and did the same to Barton. The men's eyes went completely white, then a lightless black, and finally back to normal—but something had changed in them. They stared vacantly, as if due to an underlying soullessness.

As the frantic battle continued within the facility, the portal began to close. It began pulling in all the matter around it. Agent Hill estimated that they had thirteen minutes before the entire compound would be sucked into the portal's vacuum.

Barton aimed an arrow, but his target was not what the S.H.I.E.L.D. agents might have expected—it was trained on Colonel Fury. It was clear that their enemy's staff had some strange affect on Barton. He let his arrow fly, and it flew straight into Fury's Kevlar vest.

With Barton holding Fury at bay, the infiltrator grabbed the Tesseract and, together with Selvig and

Barton, fled the compound and raced into an SUV. Agent Hill radioed any and all S.H.I.E.L.D. agents who might receive her message. One of S.H.I.E.L.D.'s best agents and a brilliant scientist had just escaped with the Tesseract, accompanied by a powerful being who could only be Loki, son of Odin, brother of Thor.

Hill rushed out toward the parking structure. The fugitives were still in sight, so she jumped in her own SUV and gave chase. She sped through the complex's labyrinthine tunnels, skidding against the walls as she followed in hot pursuit. Agent Barton fired shots at Hill from the enemy vehicle, but Hill couldn't help but note that he was less accurate than usual.

Even so, one of Barton's arrows exploded near Agent Hill's SUV, causing it to tumble.

As Loki's vehicle emerged from the tunnel, a S.H.I.E.L.D. helicopter descended and picked up the chase where Hill had left off. Fury leaned out one of the doors and began to fire upon the escape vehicle, but the escapees managed to swerve and avoid the barrage. At the same time, Barton, with his hawklike eyes, returned fire and managed to hit a rotor on the copter, which plunged to earth.

Fury managed to escape the craft seconds before it exploded. Then he looked up as the SUV drove off with the most powerful energy source in the known universe inside.

CHAPTER TWENTY-FOUR

THIS WAS A VERY different New York City than the one Steve Rogers had known. His beloved Brooklyn Dodgers had left "the borough of churches" for the glitz and glamour of Los Angeles. Their uptown rivals, baseball's New York Giants, had also up and left for the West Coast. The spectacular adverts in Times Square—always impressive—had transformed from mechanical gimmickry to mind-blowing high-tech LED lights. The skyline had nearly doubled its height during the time he'd been away. Subways were faster—and cleaner. Traffic was more congested than ever, but the cars were sleeker. Gone were the phone booths—people now carried personal phones that had no need for wires. And these devices were not merely used for speaking, but also watching films, reading books, listening to music, and sending and receiving information instantaneously.

Steve was reminded of Howard Stark's vision of the future at the World Exposition that had changed Steve's life back in 1941. Steve was sure that in no small way, Howard was responsible for many of these great advancements.

This was the new world outside of Steve's apartment window. Inside, Colonel Fury had used new technologies to supply Steve with everything he needed to familiarize himself with the new world in which he found himself. It was jarring to emerge from the mid twentieth century into the twenty-first. To make the leap from never having seen a television to fidgeting with a tablet device would not be easy. Steve needed to know about everything that had come in between.

He started from the beginning, watching old news-reels of himself in battle during the war. He shook his head in disbelief at how crude and unsophisticated the film and sound were compared to what he'd recently seen—flat crystal-clear screens where it seemed as though you could reach out and grab the images.

He shifted his attention to old war-era files. He sifted through them until he reached the file that mattered most—Peggy Carter, who was alive and living in

London. What would Peggy think of him now? What would he think of her?

Overwhelmed, Steve stepped out of his apartment into this brave new world. He needed to clear his mind and process all this. The street was not conducive to deep thinking. Traffic jammed the roads, street vendors shouted from their carts, tourists clogged the sidewalks. He needed to find somewhere to sit down. The bars were too crowded and depressing. Besides, he didn't drink. He thought about a coffee shop, but still couldn't find it within himself to pay more than a few cents for a cup of the stuff, no less a hundred times that, which seemed to be the going rate.

Steve found himself by Stark Tower—the legacy of his old friend Howard Stark. He looked up at the tower in awe. Almost nothing in his time looked so tall and sleek. He shook his head and sighed, then he settled into a diner across the street. The scene felt much more familiar than any of his other options.

"You waiting to see him?" the waitress asked as she set down his water.

"Who?"

"Iron Man. People come in and sit here all day

waiting to see him fly by. You can stay here all day, too," she said with a flirtatious smile. "We have free Wi-Fi," she continued.

"Is that radio?" Steve asked naively.

The waitress flashed her pretty smile again and shook her head.

"Get her number, you moron!" an old man at the table across from him snapped.

But Steve just ordered, finished up, and uncomfortably thanked the waitress for her service as he paid the bill. He was frustrated as ever with his place in the world. He'd tried walking, sitting, and thinking, there was only one other option open to him.

Steve pounded and pounded and pounded on the punching bag that hung from the gym's ceiling. He came here when all else failed—when he was out of options for how to deal with all the information he'd been having difficulty processing.

He thought of his fellow soldiers and hit the bag. He thought of Peggy and slammed it again. He thought of Howard Stark, of progress, advancement, of the seventy years of history he'd not been a part of and punched and punched and punched; harder and harder, faster and more furious.

He would have beaten that bag forever if he hadn't been interrupted by the last man in the world he wanted to see at this moment—the man who was to blame for the fact that Steve was here at all—Colonel Fury.

Fury told Steve that the Tesseract had been stolen. Steve knew all too well the destruction that could be wrought if the power of the cube fell into the wrong hands. He'd seen the destruction it caused when the Red Skull held it. What if someone smarter and more dangerous got hold of it? Fury knew from his research in S.H.I.E.L.D. databases that Steve put himself before no one. No matter what Steve was struggling with, if the world needed Captain America, he would rise to meet the challenge.

"I've left a debriefing packet at your apartment," Fury said. Then he turned and left the gym.

CHAPTER TWENTY-FIVE

HALFWAY AROUND the world in a desolate factory district in St. Petersburg, Russia, Natasha Romanoff found herself tied to a chair and interrogated by three nasty-looking goons. She was not in good shape. The agent's beautiful but deadly ways had earned her the codename Black Widow. But right now, it seemed as if she were closer to dead than deadly.

One of the thug's phones began to ring, and he answered.

"This is agent Coulson of S.H.I.E.L.D. We know your exact coordinates and will not have a second thought descending on you if you don't hand Ms. Romanoff the phone right now."

The thug quickly obliged.

"What is it? I'm working," Natasha told Coulson. "Hold on."

Natasha shimmied her way out of the ropes that had been binding her and quickly and easily knocked out her captors. Once she was certain they were out of commission, she again picked up the phone.

"I was getting good information out of these guys. Where do you need me?"

Coulson filled Natasha in on the Tesseract threat. There was no way that S.H.I.E.L.D. or any one hero would be able to handle this situation on their own. He told her that Barton had been compromised, which caused Natasha to listen up and take the call even more seriously.

"We need you to bring in the big guy," Coulson said.

"Tony Stark trusts me as far as he can throw me," Natasha said.

"No, I've got Stark," Coulson said. "The *BIG* guy."

Natasha took a deep breath. "Oh, boy."

This wasn't going to be easy. Even for the Black Widow.

CHAPTER TWENTY-SIX

THE NEW YORK CITY skyline glittered. The bridges sparkled like strings of pearls in the reflective waters of the East River. In recent years, the skyline had been built back up from darker days at the turn of the millennium. But even with the explosion of construction the city was experiencing, one tower was sure to stand out above all the others.

Like a cannon fired from a submarine, Iron Man shot from below the surface of the river and soared into the sparkling sky over Manhattan.

The PR campaign had been a success, the media outlets were alerted, and Stark Industries' CEO was ready to flip the switch. Tonight was the night they lit Stark Tower—New York's newest and most spectacular skyscraper, and its most eco-friendly: the first in not just the city, but the world to run on self-sustaining energy.

Tony gave Pepper the word, and his CEO activated the building's power. The tower began to light up, first from street level, and then hundreds of feet to the pinnacle, illuminating the New York skyline—and the sky itself.

"Woo-hoo!" Tony cheered.

Back at the tower, Pepper smiled proudly.

The event was a success! Pepper was surrounded by press, and Tony was soaring around the lit skyscraper, relishing the moment.

Of course, for Tony, it was never quite that easy to relax.

"Sir, Agent Coulson is on the line for you," J.A.R.V.I.S. said through the communications line in Tony's helmet.

Without responding, Tony hung up on the automated butler. This feeling was too great to let Coulson and the rest of his S.H.I.E.L.D. cronies spoil it.

Tony flew back to the tower, and its penthouse suite, where Pepper was waiting for him. He gave her *some* of the credit for the evening's success, but the rest of it was, of course, all him.

Just then a video screen lit up, and on it appeared

Agent Coulson. He'd overridden J.A.R.V.I.S.'s secutity protocols.

"Tony, I need to speak with you urgently," Coulson said.

Tony switched off the screen, and as if on cue the elevator doors to the penthouse opened and Coulson stepped out. There was no avoiding this guy.

Tony sighed. "Security."

Coulson handed Tony a briefcase. "I need you to look at this as soon as possible."

Tony refused to take it, but Pepper, not quite sure exactly what to do, grabbed it for him.

"I thought Fury had scrapped this whole Avengers Initiative thing," Tony said. "And anyway, I didn't qualify."

Coulson explained that the threat they were facing now was so great that they would need all the help they could get. This wasn't the Avengers Initiative, it was a response team.

Semantics, Tony thought.

Pepper shushed Tony and took him into an adjoining room, where they opened up the briefcase. Inside were holographic images containing information on

Captain America, Hulk, Thor, and Tony himself. But most impressive of all was the Tesseract. Tony had an idea of what is was and what it could do. And how, if it fell into the wrong hands, it could spell disaster. In the hands of a madman, the entire world would be at risk. In the hands of something greater than human, there was no telling where or if the devastation would end.

CHAPTER TWENTY-SEVEN

BRUCE BANNER leaned over his two young patients as their worried mother looked on. Calcutta was fraught with pestilence. But Bruce was intent on making sure that the children he was currently tending to would grow up to experience the world and, hopefully, make it a better place.

Calcutta suffered from a dearth of critical needs, such as freshwater, medicine, and other supplies. Unfortunately the one thing there was no shortage of was patients. Just as Banner was wrapping up his work, a young girl who couldn't have been more than eight years old ran into the home.

"Stay away!" The mother cried out. "They're sick!"

The girl explained that she was here because her father was sick in the same way. She burst into tears and continued the story as her voice broke with sorrow.

"He's not waking up," she told Banner. "He has a fever and is moaning, but his eyes won't open."

She held out the little bit of money she had and offered it to Bruce, pleading for his help. He didn't accept the money, but still threw his supplies into his worn doctor's bag and asked the girl to show him the way to her father.

They made their way through the nearly impenetrable Calcutta streets. The girl knew better than Bruce how to navigate the thick walls of people, but Bruce did his best to keep up with the girl, so as not to lose her.

They arrived at the very edge of town, which was a much less densely populated than the rest of the city. The girl led Bruce to a shack that stood apart from the others. It was even more severely dilapidated than the rest. She darted into the shack and Bruce, still trying to keep pace, followed right behind her.

Once inside the shanty, the girl rushed quickly onto a bed beneath a window. And then she slipped right through that window out of the room.

It took Bruce a few seconds to register what was going on, but then he realized what had happened. He'd been tricked.

A beautiful S.H.I.E.L.D. agent stood before him. The jig was up—they'd been looking for him for years, and now they had him.

The woman introduced herself as Natasha Romanoff.

"How did S.H.I.E.L.D. find me?" Banner asked.

"We never lost you," Natasha responded. "I'm here, alone, on behalf of S.H.I.E.L.D. We need you to come in."

Natasha said S.H.I.E.L.D. was aware it had been two years without an incident. They weren't looking for the Hulk, they needed Bruce Banner. She explained that the Tesseract was stolen, possibly by a being once worshiped as a god. They needed to find it before he could use its power, but it was emitting gamma radiation that was too weak for any of their tools to trace. Bruce was the world's leading expert on gamma radiation, and they needed that expert advice right now.

Banner didn't believe it. He still thought that S.H.I.E.L.D. wanted the Hulk, not Banner.

"Stop lying to me!" he shouted with a vehement anger.

Natasha, who was not easily jarred, was startled out of her wits, bracing herself for Banner's transformation into the Hulk.

Then Bruce began to laugh. "That was mean!" he said. "Couldn't resist. What if I say no?"

"Then I will persuade you," Natasha replied.

"What if the *other* guy says no?"

Bruce's question met an uncomfortable silence as both he and Natasha considered what would happen if the Hulk decided that he didn't want to go along with S.H.I.E.L.D. Finally, Bruce spoke up. "If Fury wants me, we both know he's going to get me either way," he said, agreeing to come along.

"The situation is contained," Natasha said into her walkie-talkie.

"So we were alone, huh?" Bruce said.

Natasha shrugged while, outside, thirty-odd S.H.I.E.L.D. agents who'd surrounded the shack dropped their weapons.

CHAPTER TWENTY-EIGHT

SILENCE. That's all Agent Coulson could provide his hero, his idol, this man he never thought it possible that he'd meet. Steve Rogers sat across from Agent Coulson on a high-tech aircraft called the Quinjet. Even though the ride was smooth as silk, Coulson found himself more than a little bit uncomfortable. But the discomfort was mutual. Coulson was starstruck, in awe, blown away. And Steve wasn't used to such adoration. During the war he wore a mask and rarely came face-to-face with the general public. But Coulson was sitting here, looking him in the eyes, or at least trying to.

Finally, the S.H.I.E.L.D. agent brought himself to make some small talk, which evolved into a very lively conversation that he was loathe to end when the Quinjet landed on S.H.I.E.L.D.'s Helicarrier. The men stepped off the Quinjet on to the carrier, where they were greeted by Natasha and Bruce.

Bruce, like everyone else, was in particular awe of Steve Rogers—the famous Captain America—and took full advantage of the opportunity to speak to a living legend, one who technically wasn't even living just a short time ago. Bruce was fascinated with the details of Steve's cryonic suspension. Though Steve couldn't give many details, Bruce found any and all that could be shared fascinating. All the while, Natasha kept to herself, typically brooding, preferring to keep to the shadows. But if anyone knew her well—which none present really did—it would be clear that something was not sitting well with her.

The gears on the carrier began to shift, and the entire ship started to rumble. The passengers were prepared for the ship to submerge—like a huge submarine—but instead the entire massive carrier lifted up into the air. Photo-variant panels on the underside of the Helicarrier reflected the sky, and cloaked the ship, rendering it completely invisible. The sound was roaring, but it suddenly cut off as a noise-cancelling device was activated just as Colonel Fury entered the area.

"Thank you all for coming," he said. He turned to Banner who of all the heroes was looking the most uncomfortable. "As soon as the Tesseract is back in S.H.I.E.L.D.'s hands, you can go. I'm not going to keep you here."

Bruce smiled uncomfortably, only half believing Fury.

"The cube is emitting gamma radiation, and no one knows about that better than you," Fury said.

Coulson informed Banner that S.H.I.E.L.D. had access to any device connected to a satellite. That access would be made available to Banner. Bruce let Coulson know that he'd also need spectrometers. Fury quickly ordered a lab to be set up for Banner, and he supplied him not only with spectrometers, but an endless supply of other devices that could be used to track the Tesseract.

Before long, Bruce was working. In no time at all, a hot spot appeared in Stuttgart, Germany.

"Got it!" Banner shouted.

The group boarded the Quinjet and was on its way immediately. More forces were gathering. They'd need all the power they could assemble to fight this battle.

Every second that the Tesseract was in the thief's hands was another second during which the fate of the world hung in the balance.

The battle was about to begin.

CHAPTER TWENTY-NINE

IN A SQUARE outside a museum in Stuttgart, Germany, an. unassuming man carrying a walking stick strode by a string quartet. The man meandered about a bit, taking in the evening, enjoying the night and the music. He surveyed the museum and walked around its perimeter, admiring its architecture and expressing interest in the evening's event. He eventually made his way around to the rear. Once he was sure no one was looking, he slipped inside through a back entrance.

Inside the museum, a speaker was delivering a science lecture. The man who had sneaked in appeared at the top of the grand staircase behind the speaker and began to descend. As he stepped down the stairs, his long coat and walking stick morphed into the unmistakable battle armor and staff of Loki the Trickster.

Loki was on the run, but he still couldn't resist using his powers on the inhabitants of Midgard. Loki began firing bolts of energy from his staff every which way. Then he stepped out the front doors as gracefully as he'd entered.

A guard, hearing the disturbance but not knowing who or what had caused it, raced up to Loki as he exited the museum. He was intent on stopping him.

"Kneel!" Loki commanded the guard.

The guard collapsed onto his knees before Loki.

Suddenly it appeared as though Loki was multiplying —dozens of him filled the square.

"All of you, kneel!" He shouted to the people in the square.

Everyone dropped to their knees, except for one man who stood out conspicuously in the crowd.

"I do not kneel to men like you," the old man said.

"There are no men like me," Loki replied.

"There are *always* men like you," the old man retorted.

Loki lifted his staff and pointed it at the man in disgust. He fired a bolt of energy. Then, suddenly, seemingly from nowhere at all, a loud clang reverberated.

Something swooped by in a blur and ricocheted off of the energy stream—deflecting Loki's blast and keeping the old man from harm, then swiping Loki across the head as it swooped back toward its wielder.

It was the shield of Captain America, and it had been a very long time since it had been used to fight the good fight.

"Ah, the Super-Soldier from the Great War," Loki said.

"It wasn't that 'great,'" Captain America replied flatly.

"Mine will be," Loki said evilly.

Meanwhile, in the air above, Natasha was piloting the Quinjet. Her objective was to stun Loki with a blast, but the square was too crowded. She needed it to be cleared before she could get a clean shot.

"I'll get this one," Cap said, facing down Loki.

The two began to spar all over the square, Loki dodging the Captain's shield, Cap bouncing back every time Loki dealt him a blow. All the while, Natasha attempted to fix a target on Loki, but he darted around far too quickly to be locked down.

Troublingly, Natasha's radio filled with static. No, it

wasn't static, it was . . . heavy metal music? Then she realized what was happening.

"Hello, Tony," she said.

Iron Man zoomed past the Quinjet and swooped down to the square, where he began to fire repulsor blasts at Loki. Loki persisted, but Tony trained his repulsor ray on Loki's staff and blasted it out of his hand. The staff skittered down the square. Still, Loki would not relent. He continued to battle both Captain America and Iron Man. But then, the latter descended into the square, hovered in front of Loki and transformed his armor to show that the suit was outfitted with every Stark Industries weapon imaginable— including some that no one else could even conjure in their wildest dreams.

Loki threw up his hands in defeat, an evil smile on his face.

"Good move," Tony said, then he turned to the man with the shield.

"Mr. Stark," Steve said.

"Captain."

CHAPTER THIRTY

BACK IN THE Quinjet, Natasha, Tony, and Steve stood sentry over Loki. Fury radioed in, telling them to get Loki to the S.H.I.E.L.D. Helicarrier. They'd continue the search for the Tesseract later. The main thing was to make sure it wasn't in Loki's hands and that he was kept in a place where he could do no more harm.

Natasha was at the controls, piloting the Quinjet and watching as dark black clouds rolled in over the jet under an otherwise crystal clear sky.

"Where's this coming from?" she said. The clouds began to ripple with lightning, and a low, rolling thunder sounded, rattling the jet.

At first the group thought that Loki was responsible. But that didn't appear to be the case. He looked more nervous than anyone else on the jet.

"What's the matter?" Cap asked. "You scared of lightning?"

"I'm not overly fond of what follows," Loki replied.

A loud crack of thunder punctuated Loki's remark, and the group could feel something huge and powerful land on top of the jet. Captain America and Iron Man suited up, preparing to respond. From a jet cam, Natasha could see a man in full battle armor that she immediately recognized from S.H.I.E.L.D. files as Thor standing on top of the jet, illuminated by the lightning that crashed around him.

Iron Man ordered the gangway of the Quinjet to be lowered so he could fly out and respond.

"Wait! He might be friendly!" Captain America warned.

"Doesn't matter, if he's come to rescue our prisoner."

As the ramp began to open and Iron Man prepared to jet out, huge, strong hands wedged into the opening and pried the ramp open the rest of the way.

Stunned, Iron Man held up his hands to fire a repulsor blast, but before he could act, Thor flung Mjolnir at Iron Man, sending him cascading across the Quinjet into Captain America. With Iron Man and Captain

America out of commission, Thor grabbed his brother. Mjolnir returned to Thor, who raised it and used it to flee from the Quinjet with Loki in tow.

Iron Man and Captain America looked at each other in disbelief. Then Tony did the only thing there was to do in a situation like this—he rocketed out of the ship.

Steve was amazed at the speed at which Tony moved. He grabbed a parachute and strapped it on.

Natasha looked at him skeptically. They were thousands of feet above land, the Quinjet was moving at a supersonic clip, and—as far as she knew—Captain America couldn't fly.

"Um, maybe you should sit this one out," she said.

Cap just turned to Natasha, saluted her, and jumped out of the plane.

Meanwhile, the Asgardian brothers had alighted on a mountainside, and Thor, now the more diplomatic of the two, continued his never-ending quest to understand his brother.

"With the Bifrost destroyed, Odin must have used all his power to get you here," Loki said.

"We thought you were dead. We mourned. Our father . . ."

"*Your* father!" Loki replied. "Did he not tell you my true parentage?"

"Loki, we were raised together. Played together. Fought together. Do you remember *none* of this?"

"What I remember is growing up in your shadow," Loki said bitterly.

"You must return to Asgard. We will talk to the Allfather. . . ."

"I am not going anywhere. If Asgard can't be mine, then I shall rule over Midgard," Loki said, becoming increasingly incensed.

"You know nothing of ruling," Thor shouted back.

Just as the exchange between the two gods was reaching a fever pitch, something shot from the air and plowed into Thor, knocking him clear out of the scene: it was the Invincible Iron Man. Thor responded in kind, and the two heroes battled violently. Tony's circuitry started to go haywire, due to the interference caused by Thor's lightning. Thor wailed upon Iron Man's armor with Mjolnir, rocking Tony with blow after blow. Every time Tony picked himself up, Thor knocked him back down. With every blow, it became more difficult for Tony to pick himself back up. He and his armor were taking a beating, and his armor was shutting down.

Thor was growing weary of Tony's resistance. He had a feeling Iron Man could go on taking a beating all day and never stay down. So Thor raised Mjolnir and summoned all the power available to him, causing a great column of lightning to descend from the skies and jolt Tony's armor with an unearthly clap of power and energy.

Inside Tony's suit, J.A.R.V.I.S. alerted Tony that the lightning had fed the suit with an unprecedented power surge, and his power was now at 400-percent. Tony shot up and blasted Thor with a repulsor blast that knocked the Mighty Thor down and kept the battle alive. Thor picked himself up. Before turning his attention back to Iron Man, he shot a warning glance toward Loki, letting him know he should not even think about trying to flee. Thor wasn't done with him yet.

As the two superpowered beings faced off again, something shot down between them, blocking any further aggression. Tony turned to see Captain America with his shield raised, urging diplomacy.

In response, Thor swung Mjolnir over his head and slammed it at Captain America. But Cap was quick to block the hammer with his shield, resulting in an unearthly sonic BOOM!

All four men on the mountain were knocked back by the shockwave from the collision.

"Are we done here?" Captain America asked as the vibrations subsided.

The three heroes looked over toward Loki, the reason they were battling. The god of mischief smirked. Thor grabbed his brother and brought him back to the Quinjet, where he would force the Trickster to cooperate with S.H.I.E.L.D. It was what needed to be done after what Thor had learned about his brother's desire to conquer Earth.

Once S.H.I.E.L.D. had what it needed from Loki, Thor would return his brother to Asgard, where he was sure to pay for his ways.

EPILOGUE

BACK ON THE S.H.I.E.L.D. Helicarrier, Bruce Banner watched as Loki was locked up in a huge glass cage.

"This wasn't meant for me, you know," Loki taunted Bruce through the video surveillance. "It was constructed for someone angrier and greener."

Bruce sensed his heart rate increasing as Loki antagonized him. He breathed deeply to settle down.

Loki hissed at Colonel Fury. He wouldn't be held so easily.

But Fury argued that point. The colonel showed that there was no way out on any of the cell's sides. He flipped a switch and the floor slid open, revealing a glass enclosure over a 30,000-foot drop. If Loki tried to escape, the doors of the glass floor would part, and Loki would plunge to Earth.

Agent Coulson radioed in that the Tesseract, Agent Barton, and Dr. Selvig had been located. The two men had been brainwashed by Loki. With Loki defeated, the effects of his hypnosis were wearing off, and the Tesseract was on its way back to S.H.I.E.L.D.'s carrier.

Loki was trapped and the world was safe, at least for the moment. Thor stood aboard the Helicarrier, waiting to return his brother to Asgard to face Odin's strong arm of justice.

Bruce, Steve, Natasha, and Tony each looked at one another and then over at Thor. None of them could have captured Loki alone. It was only together—despite their rocky start—that they were able to prevent certain disaster.

This was the first, but surely not the final time that the great Super Heroes of the world had come together and assembled into a team. It was the start of something incredible, invincible . . . and mighty. It was the beginning of an initiative that Nick Fury had tried to assemble for years, despite facing obstacles every step of the way. But with the fate of the world, perhaps the universe, hanging in the balance, Earth's

Mightiest Heroes had come together to protect, to serve, to defend, and to avenge.

And as Colonel Fury watched Loki contemplate his cell and Thor ready his brother for a trip back to Asgard, he realized that if the world ever again needed them, they would band together again.

Whenever duty called, the Avengers would answer—for now and forever, fighting for the greatest good and never relenting till the battle was won.